THE CASE OF THE
ENSLAVED SOULS

THE CASE OF THE ENSLAVED SOULS

JAMES E. BEKSHA

ARPress
45 Dan Road Suite 5
Canton MA 02021

Hotline: 1(888) 821-0229
Fax: 1(508) 545-7580

Ordering Information:
Quantity sales. Special discounts are available on quantity purchases by corporations, associations, and others. For details, contact the publisher at the address above.

Printed in the United States of America.

ISBN-13:   Softcover   979-8-89356-331-3
            eBook   979-8-89356-332-0

Library of Congress Control Number: 2024905480

DEDICATION

There are four people I'd like to dedicate this book to. However, before I do that, I'd like to say thank you, first, to all the doubters and naysayers out there who thought and have said I was wasting my time. You kept my creative fire burning with your negative comments.

Now, to the First Person I happily dedicate this book to, his name is Bruno J. Beksha. My Grandfather. He was a very strong man who taught me there was nothing you can't do when you put your mind to it…and knew I believed it.

The Second Person I'd like to dedicate this is to my Uncle Bernard J. Beksha Sr. My Uncle taught me to always believe in myself and never give up on what makes you happy.

The Third Person I dedicate this is to my cousin, Annette L. Beksha. My cousin taught me to fight and never quit. It's funny whenever I thought about quitting in my pursuit to become a writer. I always close my eyes and see my cousin in my mind shaking her head "no" to me in her special way and that, always, kept me going.

The Fourth and final person I'd like to dedicate this book to is to my father, William A. Beksha. He teaches me to be the best I can be and do the best I can. "You know something; it took me twenty-two years to learn how to study hard in chasing what I wanted to accomplish by being a fiction writer. Shame I couldn't have developed this habit in high school, huh, dad?"

In Closing, let me leave you with this, my friend…

"Never Quit Chasing what makes you happy doing.
Never Stop Believing in yourself, and, last but certainly
not least, Never Ever Stop Rocking it."

God bless you, everybody.

Someone once said

"Every writer has one weird story they need to
get out of them before they can write their better stuff."

—Guess this is mine

PROLOGUE

Case of the Enslaved Souls

Brenda walked slowly moving thru the dim lit corridor being led by the strange man in front of her. A black leather collar was snugly placed around her neck attached thru its single hole was a lengthy leash clipped to it; her naked body glistened with sweat from her very first session.

She could only remember fragments as the grin upon her face still displayed there.

Escorted into a completely different room with other exceptionally beautiful ladies all kneeling reciting a kind of mantra.

It wouldn't be until having the collar and leash taken off her that she had two ear buds firmly placed within her ears.

Gently feeling the man pushed her down caused Brenda to start kneeling herself slowly and she began reciting what the others were saying

"I Have no mind, I have no will, I will obey." Hence began her conditioning.

The daughter of Mr. Alan Davis, a research scientist for the Government D.O.D. Shortly after 12 straight hours of an intense and unique style of torture sadly gave up her father's secret start up codes to his highly sensitive defense system. Which under any normal circumstance Brenda would not have imagined herself doing.

CHAPTER ONE

Monday morning, June 8th 1990 saw me walking down the hallway of Boston Police headquarters for a special meeting with my Uncle Jesse.

I dressed today for this meeting somewhat formally, not that anyone would've noticed.

I had on a pair of black slacks, a white silk shirt a red tie, and blue blazer.

Also, my sliver tipped cowboy boots that could be heard in unison with the rest of the officers of the precinct.

Walking toward my Uncles office a few of the detectives and uniforms who had seen me either stopped to say hello, or they'd shake my hand, as they passed by.

To tell you truth I was sort of toying with a notion that this meeting might end up with me getting hired to find a possible missing person.

After all; I have been pretty obsessed with this strange abduction case for a while. If you don't believe me just ask my wife Lori-Ann.

She'd either see me watching the coverage intensely on television, or noticed me down in my basement office reading about it in various newspapers and periodicals I'd buy just to keep myself updated with it.

And with this past weekend's disappearance of Brenda Davis from her downtown Boston apartment.

You could say I was literally jumping at the chance to get into this investigation big time.

Initially this all started two and a half years ago around this time out in California with the loveliest of young women just disappearing without a trace baffling state and local authorities beyond belief as to where they would've gone.

But even more bizarre than each of their disappearances was the crime scene evidence discovered.

Whoever this was always places two articles inside of an oversized manila envelope.

The first article was always a totally nude photograph of each of the victims in a head to toe shot followed immediately by a strange single lined message that always read.

"One more added to the fold" Scratching their heads like I said before authorities did the best they could with what little evidence they had to process.

But really who knew this would only be the beginning because other states across the country quickly began to experience the same bizarre occurrences as well.

Massachusetts up until this past weekend was one of the last states to have been spared by this bizarre epidemic.

Catching the site of the name plate out of my right eye it simply read: "Jesse James Police Commissioner"

Turning slowly, I felt a subtle smile come over me as I stood before the door. I momentarily thought about him being first promoted to that prominent position by his honor the Mayor. I remember watching him; smiling; winking; over at me then giving me the thumbs up which I gave right back.

Shaking my head to awaken from my reverie, I knocked on his door listening I heard him call out to "come in"

Excusing himself he got up from behind his desk and walked over to greet me as I entered. He stood 5'10" tall and had a good muscular build for a man his age.

I noticed he had on the same style shirt as I had on with a blue/white uniform type tie, also a darker blue blazer hanging up beside the desk on his coat rack just to my left. He also had on black slacks that Lori-Ann and I had given him last Christmas with the creases perfectly pressed.

Uncle Jesse gave me a long hug which I might add isn't weird in the least and hugging him back, as I did my eyes fell upon another gentleman also in the room with us.

I immediately recognized the gentleman as Mr. Alan Davis having read an article about him in a news magazine. It said he was the developer of a computerized strategic defense control system, the very first of its kind.

He looked to be around my Uncle's age, maybe a bit younger; he had on a pair of jeans, a Grey pocket t-shirt, and brown boat shoes. I noticed he had a black brief case on the floor beside his chair on the right. It wouldn't be until making myself a coffee that we would walk over to join his guest.

His friend naturally rose up slightly in respect to my approaching to take my seat just to his left.

After placing my cup down on the corner of my Uncle's desk I sensed a nervousness about the man.

Looking toward Uncle Jesse, his eyes were calm, but I had a stronger than average feeling something was wrong in the room.

"Eddie, first off I'd like to thank you for coming in today for this meeting and I'd like to add that I do apologize for taking you away from anything you were busy with."

Slowly shaking my head my Uncle watched me with the subtlest of smiles as I replied, "You're very welcome Uncle Jesse, it's an honor for me to be asked to be here for you, and please—you never have to apologize for taking me away from anything I'm doing." Having said that we each saluted the other with raising our coffee mugs.

"Before I go ahead and explain why I asked you here Eddie, I'd first like to introduce you to my old college roommate Alan Davis, Alan this is my nephew Eddie James I told you about him the other day you remember?" Turning slightly, I extended my hand to him. He accepted shaking it quickly without much of a grip. Only confirming to me as he took it back that something was indeed wrong.

"Alan Please! Remember what we discussed; Eddie please accept my apology for my friend's rudeness. It's just he's been here since Saturday frantic with worry about his daughter who?"

"Disappeared isn't that right Uncle Jesse? And let me guess all Mr. Davis here found was a large manila envelope?" The silence that followed pretty much meant it was true.

While I continued sitting there drinking my coffee: my thoughts turned to the unimaginable concept of possibly getting hired by Mr. Davis to locate his missing daughter for him. Turning his head away from us Mr. Davis tried to conceal from our view a lone tear that was trickling down his cheek, but not meaning to I quickly spotted it. "Pardon me Mr. Davis for not taking."

Watching him holding up his hand I gave him a minute before replying back to me. "Please Eddie, you don't have to apologize to me, but you were right though; I did indeed receive a large manila envelope actually it was conveniently placed on my rental car's windshield."

Uncle Jesse and I continued to watch Mr. Davis trying to recompose himself more, before continuing to tell us about the events that transpired upon his arriving to Boston.

"Let's see I arrived at Logan Airport about nine o' clock, picked up my bags, rented my car then drove to my hotel to freshen up before going over to see Brenda."

"What hotel were you staying at?"

"Oh, the Four Seasons Eddie; Sorry I'm just a bit nervous." "That's all right Sir you're doing fine isn't he Uncle Jesse?" "Yes, Alan you're doing fine please continue my friend."

"Thanks, well after checking in I decided to take a nap before going over to surprise her."

My immediate impression of him was that he was indeed dedicated to not only his work with the Government, but his daughter as well.

I mean come on if you were a government employee, and your only child was moving away to a new city wouldn't you be a bit worried about exactly where she was living too, or for that matter if the neighborhood she found herself moving into was safe.

"Let's see I found myself next waking up around eleven to prepare for my drive over to see her; she described where she was living in a phone conversation a couple of days prior to my arriving. As a nice neighborhood from her building with the Boston Common and the State house directly across the street."

Knowing exactly what street his friend was referring to Uncle Jesse and I could be seen nodding our heads together.

"That's Tremont St. Alan, Eddie and I know exactly the building your talking about it's a three-story building owned by Mrs. Gladys Preston. She rents apartments on the second and third floors, according to one of my officer's reports Brenda lived on the third floor of that building isn't that right?" Nodding his head toward us he next exclaimed.

"Yes Jesse, Brenda did mention that to me over the phone, eventually I did manage to get there parking across the street, and I did meet Mrs. Preston who in my opinion was the nicest landlady I ever met before. She heard my name and immediately brought me up to Brenda's apartment chatting with me as we went about how friendly she was."

Hesitating for a moment before continuing his facial expression changed suggesting to us he was in a reflective moment, smiling to myself I knew exactly when those kinds of things would hit me too, so it wasn't any trouble sitting there waiting for him to continue. "Oh, wow sorry about that guys I was just."

Slightly embarrassed by the moment that did occur we completely understood not feeling the bit offended.

"Once inside the apartment I just simply looked around at all her unpacked boxes stacked on top of the other.

Knowing just how much work it might have been to completely move in it certainly didn't surprise me the least; that she hadn't gotten around to un-packing.

My guess is she was so exhausted, knowing my daughter, she could have taken off to the beach for all I knew.

So, I just left thinking to myself that could've been the reason she wasn't there.

Anyway, after returning the key back to Mrs. Preston I thanked her for being so gracious, and proceeded across the street to my car now this is the part where it gets weird."

Together we watched Mr. Davis reaching down to bring up his brief case from the floor continuing to watch him opening it he then pulls out a large manila envelope that he proceeds to place on the corner of my Uncle Jesse's desk.

"I spotted my rental across the street from her building with this attached to my windshield wiper. Knowing exactly what it stood for naturally it wouldn't be until taken it off there. Before I next saw myself opening it to view its horrific contents. Sure, enough there was a color photograph of my daughter in a?"

Meaning to say in a head to toe shot Uncle Jesse and I completely knew what he wanted to tell us. So, we excused him from not being able to continue speaking instead we sat there as his pent-up emotions finally took hold of him crying there in front of us.

It took several additional minutes more before we watched him recomposing himself.

But once he had he immediately apologized which to us given the gravity of the situation wasn't necessary. But still we waited until he was finished after he said.

"Aside from my crying about it guy's that's pretty much my situation since I arrived here, so Jesse about that conversation we had the other night. I know and completely understand your position with the police department here. But do you think he could help me find her?" It suddenly occurred to me why I was invited to this meeting.

But yes, if you were to ask me if I was shocked the answer was pretty evident by the smile on my face. After which not only does Mr. Davis present me with a retainer check, but also that large manila envelope.

Never one to pass up a golden opportunity like this upon accepted that manila envelope Mr. Davis and I shook hands once more.

This time his grip felt firmer, and just a bit more confident than before as we each smiled at one another again.

It wouldn't be until thanking my uncle also that I shook his hand in appreciation of his confidence in me.

Not until his office door closed behind me that I next could be seen pumping my fist in the air in silent celebration as to my officially being on the clock and ready to rock.

Thinking back to previous conversations we'd have together I never imagined in my wildest dreams my uncle would ever assist me like this. But seeing that he had, I was more determined than ever not to disappoint him.

My first move should've been to deposit the retainer check into our bank account.

But given the fact I was already at police headquarters it made much more sense for me to checkout Miss Davis's car out first. It certainly didn't matter who you were today; going from an air-conditioned building to the humidity outside was just like getting hit with a proverbial wet blanket.

With my tie undone a little I slung my blazer over my arm then continued walking toward the impound yard. The yard as its best called measured the length of two football fields with every make and model imaginable parked behind the precinct.

Fortunately, Brenda's car was at the beginning where most of the newer tows were, once there brought into the yard. Immediately after flashing my badge toward the attendant he handed me the keys to Brenda's car. Her car was a very old school Ford Mustang Boss 351 with a Windsor engine. Its interior was black with plush seat covers.

And its exterior was painted canary yellow with a black stripe down either side of its doors it also had a very stylish hood scoop on it as well.

After giving its exterior a careful look, I turned my attention to its interior next. Upon opening its driver's door my senses were knock back a bit from the aroma of cleaning solvents that hit me.

The first thing I noticed was it did have plush seat coverings not only in the front and back seat areas, but it also had the same carpeting on its flooring too. Brenda's agenda looked as though she was heading to the beach seeing two oversized towels in the backseat along with a container of sun tan lotion and a large bottle of water.

Turning back around there in the front it looked somewhat normal to say the least but then my eye caught site of the young lady's radar detector. Seeing only a single screw holding it on top of the dashboard caused me to make a note of it, as well as producing my camera for a photo opportunity.

After tucking my notebook into my shirt pocket then putting my camera away. I next contemplated contorting my upper body under her dashboard for a look see. But just before making my mind up to that my cell phone at that very moment started to ring. Seeing it was my wife; I more than happily took the call.

"Hey baby, what's up anything wrong?"

"Hi Honey, no, no, there's nothing wrong, I just miss you, and wanted to know how you made out at the meeting this morning?"

"Oh, gee that's sweet of you to say that I miss you also baby, and to answer your second question the meeting went well. I got hired by Mr. Davis I'm working now as a matter of fact."

"Congratulations, Mr. James."

"Why thank you Mrs. James, hey by the way what time is it?"

"Umm, it's 11:30am."

"Really your home early from school."

"Yeah, I know one of my professors had a dentist appointment, so, my last class was canceled"

"Oh, I see, so what are you going to be doing with the rest of your day while I'm working?" Knowing my wife could never resist teasing me she didn't disappoint me by replying back.

"Well, I was thinking about skinny dipping in the pool then laying out on the lounge chair to tan myself." Listening she heard me dropping my cell phone which resulted in her giggling as I bent down to pick it up.

"Sorry about that baby, phone slipped out of my hand."

"Ah huh, hey so what's the rest of your day looking like while I'm here all alone?"

"Well, after I get through here, I have to hit the bank, then touch base with Danny, and after that go checkout the young lady's apartment then I guess I'll be through for today why?"

"Oh, I just thought I'd try experimenting by barbecuing naked for a change that's all."

Like before she heard my cell phone dropping out of my hand listening I heard her giggling again into it.

"Dam Humidity, sorry about that again baby"

"It's all right honey, I'm not offended."

"Good listen baby, I'd love to keep talking to you, but I have to finish here.

But listen why don't I call you back; after I leave Miss Davis's apartment, so we can plan this barbecue thing right?"

"Sounds like a plan, I love you honey bye."

"I Love you to baby, talk to you later bye."

Smiling to myself I happily thought of my wife swimming in the pool naked; getting out; toweling herself off; then after she'd then apply some suntan lotion on her body just to lay there afterward in her lounge chair. Just baking in the sun.

Even though I may have loved to daydream about her; it certainly wasn't getting anything accomplished in my investigation. As I next could be seen leaning my upper body just under Miss Davis's dashboard. My thoughts quickly turned back to what I was originally doing.

Minutes passed before I pulled out a pair of tweezers from inside of my blazer. To retrieve that very same mounting bracket screw from her radar detector spotting it just under her accelerator pedal. I knew that a photograph along with a screw from a mounting bracket may not have been much in the way of evidence, but hey I was just getting started.

Without too much more to uncover from Miss Davis's car, I got out, locked her up, then returned the key back to the attendant, and left police headquarters.

My next stop was to our bank then after I needed to touch base with Danny Carter.

He worked as an assistant manager, at The Black Dragon Restaurant where he has been happily employed there for the past three years. But sadly, years before that he used to work for a traveling carnival and that's about the time Lori-Ann and I first met him.

It was towards the tail end of August when we found ourselves stopping to stretch our legs a bit; just taking in the sights for a while. We were heading back from Main after a much-delayed honeymoon since our marriage back on Independence Day. I had to admit though winning that giant panda bear for Lori-Ann was pretty fun, but it also was a lot harder than it looked.

Having to knock down three milk bottles off of this barrel, but I did manage to do it with my final ball. Immediately after placing her panda into the van, Lori-Ann next removed her sandals optioning to leave them there also with the bear.

Returning from there to the carnival we continued walking around once more. Having seen pretty much everything we were about to leave when together we witnessed a hence crime being committed against another human being.

A physically challenged individual who stood four and half feet tall was finding himself being bullied by two larger men who appeared to be drunk. It wouldn't be until making sure these guys couldn't see her that I next could be seen walking up to them.

Catching them both with a leg sweep I next exclaimed. "See that lady over there run to her." Without hesitation Danny did just that, as these two guys got back up to their feet.

Being as intoxicated as they obviously were I couldn't just hurt them, so while they tried to fight me I just let my speed and agility make them miss me.

Until they ran out of speed themselves and feel totally exhausted in front of me.

Luckily a police car was in the area and carted the two back to the station where they could sleep it off.

In appreciation for my saving his life Danny became our tour guide for the rest of our stay.

That being our initial first meeting we certainly kept in touch with him through phone calls at times, cards, and letters the rest of the time. But sadly, we lost touch with him figuring he may have fallen into hard times toward the end of 1985. Of course, who knew it wouldn't be until 1987 before our paths would find themselves crossing once more.

I remember it was a cold night, as I drove home through the south end my heater in my Ford Mustang was cranked to the max, as I drove past an alley. When out of my left eye I happened to have spotted a person being literally being thrown into a snow bank.

But come to find out it was someone you knew believe me it hit home. Instead of taking the chance and moving Danny myself I did the next best thing and called an ambulance. Once the E.M. T's arrived I gave them as much information as I could about Danny before they transported him to the hospital.

Immediately after which I phoned Lori-Ann to tell her what happened naturally she insisted on coming with me to the hospital. So, after making a quick pit stop home we next left to go visit Danny.

Arriving sometime later we were informed Danny hadn't been seen yet due to his not having medical insurance. So, I took out my wallet then my credit card and charged his medical care to it.

Several hours passed before a physician came out to give us an update, according to him Danny had 3 cracked ribs and a broken left arm. The doctor also suggested that Danny had to stay off his feet for six weeks which after he left did present a problem, but luckily not a big one.

Knowing his situation as a homeless person I quickly reached out to touch another friend of mine who we were hoping could help. That someone I reached out to happened to have been Sue Chang a friend of mine. Who is the proprietor and owner of The Black Dragon Restaurant who I assisted one time when a couple of hoods tried to rob her.

Ever since that incident she always tells me if I ever need a favor just to ask her. So, I was hoping that favor was still open to me. Hearing she not only had a room, but a job opportunity waiting after his recovery completely made my day upon hearing that. So ever since that time in addition to living there he was also happily employed there too. It was a little past twelve when I entered the restaurant; It was a sea of people either being seated or picking up their take-out orders.

On the good side, it most definitely made Sue Chang happy that she was this busy. On the other side of the proverbial coin it was bad for me trying to spot Danny to talk to him.

But just as I was about to call it an impossible task I suddenly felt this tug at my pant leg. Looking down smiling up at me was none other than Danny Carter himself, ushering me through the crowed we eventually made it to the kitchen area. "Wow! Danny that's some lunchtime crowd out there."

"Think so, well you should see this place after the theater gets out. Now that's a crowed you don't want to be here for believe me."

"Sounds great Danny; I'm happy you're doing well here." "Thanks pal appreciate that; so, how's Lori-Ann doing?" "Lori-Ann, she's great Danny thanks for asking."

"That's good to hear; tell her I said hello when you see her later."
"Sure, thing pal; she'll be happy to hear your doing good."

"You too from the buzz I hear congrats by the way word has it you got yourself hired to locate this Brenda Davis chick who recently disappeared."

"Yeah thanks Danny I did, but how did you know?"

"Hey your Uncle Jesse is so excited for you, and from what I hear about this cat Alan Davis, he's a very big Government scientist?"

"Yeah, he is I know pal, that's another reason why I came to see you, I'd like you to get the word out on the streets?"

"Consider it done pal I'm on it." Standing up we smiled at one another as we shook hands.

My last stop as I could be seen leaving the restaurant was to check out Brenda Davis's apartment on Tremont St.357 Tremont St was officially that last stop in my first day's investigation.

The building I was going to was owned by Gladys Preston a retired interior designer. Whose late husband Vernon originally bought the building back in the late fifties for a song. Eventually turning the three floors into affordable apartments with his wife and him living on the

first floor. They still made their money on the second and third floors up until Mr. Preston's untimely death in the winter of 1979.

Since then Mrs. Preston has continued to not only live there, but also manages the building as well in memory of her late husband.

After introducing myself it took mere minutes before she could be seen bringing me up to Miss Davis's apartment.

Once I entered to actually see them placed on top of the other suggested to me indeed her father was right in what he mentioned to us in my Uncle's office earlier.

Brenda's priorities could have been shifted slightly by the humid weather Saturday.

I next could be seen closing the door behind me as I thought to myself in reference to this past Saturday of just who'd blame her really if she did do that.

I had to admit however she did have a very nice place here, as I slowly walked around.

Seeing some clothes in a pile in the bathroom suggested to me she was there.

But then after finding a damp towel she used it suddenly happened as I picked it up off the floor. My sixth sense decided at that very moment it too wanted to join my investigation by showing me the brief images of that Saturday Brenda Davis disappeared.

The very first image I happened to see was of a sweat soaked lady carrying up a large box placing it down on the couch.

I next watched her walking over to her refrigerator only to return moments later carrying a bottle of water then seeing her plopping down on the couch completely exhausted. From there within a matter of minutes I next watched her getting back up with the bottle of water still in her hand now walking into the bathroom.

Next, I witnessed her getting undressed mere moments after this I next saw her stepping into the shower, thus explaining the towel I found myself still holding in my hand.

Minutes elapsed before she could be seen emerging with a towel wrapped around her. I then witnessed Miss Davis putting on a red thong bikini as I continued watching her with two towels over her shoulders walking dressed to kill over to the refrigerator grabbing herself some water then leaving the apartment.

Exiting as quickly as my visions appeared sometimes kind of left me afterward sweating myself, but fortunately at least I had part of the answer of where she could have gone.

It took me several minutes more before I could be seen re-emerging from her bathroom.

But once I did my course of action was to go through her boxes in her living room.

Time ticked by for me slowly with nothing yet uncovered out of the ordinary.

I mean a lot of her things I did see were young ladies apparel pretty much.

Avoiding the boxes marked kitchen written across the tops of them I had noticed three boxes marked for that room.

After re-checking my watch to see it was 3:45PM As I moved to my next box thinking it too would yield me with zero would you believe I finally hit pay dirt?

I found some photographs seeing a lot of them were just of her was one thing. But to see her in a couple with a fellow who looked identical to me that my friends is spooky. Because this very individual that had a resemblance to me was none other than my identical twin brother Elvis Aaron James.

While most were dated 1986 to the present there was one that did catch my eye the most. It was dated 12-31-89 New Year's Eve from the looks of it with its familiar background it was Times Square in New York City.

Having placed these next into an envelope I left returning the key back to Mrs. Preston I then thanked her kindly for letting me snoop.

It was now 4:00PM When I next saw myself dialing my cell phone to officially call Lori-Ann back.

As I sat in my car letting it ring she finally picked it up.

"Hello Baby"

"Hello Sweetie, Sorry, was swimming laps in the pool and couldn't hear the phone." "Oh, that explains it; all right your forgiven; this time." "Thanks, I knew you'd understand; that's why I love you."

"I Love you too baby; Listen, I just finished up here at Miss Davis's apartment So, I'm just calling to let you know I'll be home soon."

"Oh, all right, I'll get the steaks started grilling now see you soon."

"All right baby I'll be home shortly." Having disconnected with her I started my car carefully pulling back out into traffic.

Just the thought of two steaks normally made my mouth water, but just imagining them barbecued by my wife nude. Well to me that was defiantly an added bonus.

Even though I should have been off the investigative clock now; my mind believes it or not was still hard at work on a possible connection with Miss Davis and my brother.

Not meaning to I simply pulled off the road safely just long enough to look at those pictures once more.

When my sixth sense decided to kick itself in right there in the breakdown lane.

The first image this time showed my brother walking; carrying what looked like a silver tray with what I imagined looked like a drink of some kind over to her.

Seeing her smiling as he approached I next watched him handing it to gallantly to her catching the subtle wink of his eye; as he turned around.

The second image next saw the two of them coming out of a restaurant laughing together. With their arms around the others waist suggesting there really was something more to their relationship.

But then the final image I happened to see was of them at Times Square showing Elvis down on one knee with a small box opened to her.

Miss Davis's facial expression was of pure happiness as her head could be seen nodding yes toward him.

Opening my eyes after the final image faded from my site.

Left me with little doubt that my brother had indeed popped her the question there at Times Square. Which left me wondering if he knew at all his fiancé was missing yet. Taking a few more minutes before starting back out into traffic I then once it was safe to do so; did just that. After just one more stop at a local florist to pick up some roses for my wife. I once more could be seen back on the road again heading for home.

Finishing my trip within a matter of minutes pulling into the driveway. I happened to catch the scent of the steak grilling in the back filling my nostrils with their aroma; as I next saw myself stepping out of the car.

Creeping up slowly to the fence; I next couldn't help myself just to peek over it to see what else she had on the menu. Viewing her trying to side step the splattering steak juices may have been comical to see from my vantage point. But I certainly had to give Lori-Ann credit for at least making the attempt in keeping her promise she had made to me earlier. Spotted also the stainless-steel pot of its side burner; I could only imagine she had corn on the cob in there as well.

"Hello baby, Wow I'm impressed."

"Hi sweaty, how long have you been watching me long?" "Couple of minutes, hope you don't mind?"

"No, I never mind when it's you doing it; so, what do think of your chef here?"

"Hum actually I think my chef looks as delicious as those steaks on the grill right about now; but listen why don't you give me ten minutes to clean up before I sample your visual wares."

Hating like hell to have to postpone anything further from happening yet; I did indeed need to clean up first.

Within a matter of minutes; I gallantly returned with a bar of soap, a dry towel, and my bottle of shampoo.

After which Lori-Ann watches me diving into the pool next, but not before catching her licking her lips, as I came up from beneath the water.

"Ah, baby shouldn't you be watching the steaks?"

"The steaks are fine don't worry about them; besides it isn't every day I get to see a water show like this being performed by my husband."

Seeing her smiling toward me, I smiled back as I dove back into the pool once more to get all the soap off me.

Swimming back over toward her she patiently waited for me coming out of the pool next to her; I watched the gleam in her eye, as our lips softly met first.

It wouldn't be until double checking the heat on the grill, before I lifted Lori-Ann up slightly. Feeling her ankles locking themselves behind me just under my bottom. I felt her soft hands behind my neck, as I carried her over to the hammock for a little afternoon delight.

Several miles away from us however; four more ladies could be seen being tightly restrained to an extremely large table. The first young victim is Victoria Mellon an 18yr old college freshman at Florida State who found herself being abducted 5 miles or so away from campus along with her 17yr old sister.

Victoria is a stunning 6ft tall in height with a slender waist line weighing 112lbs. She has long black hair feathered back in the front. Lying directly next to her is Connie Braxton located to the right of Victoria. Connie is an Afro-American 19yr old who stands 5'11" tall in height and weighs an even more delicious 112lbs. Herself with an equally slender waist line Connie's hair was also black puffed up in a standard afro: She found herself being abducted after stopping at a traffic light.

Lying directly next to Connie is Maxine Augustine located to Connie's right side. Maxine is a 20yr old fiery red head. Who stands 6'2" tall and weighs 110lbs. She found herself abducted somewhere out in the ocean after taken out a pedal boat. Laying directly next to Maxine was the youngest casualty Tori Mellon located to Maxine's right side. She like I mentioned earlier is the 17yrs old sister of Victoria Mellon. Tori stands 5'7" tall in height; and weighs an equally slender 110lbs.

Like her sister Tori too had long black hair feathered back in the front. Carefully their attendants could be seen shaving the hair of each lady. In addition to their pleasure areas between their legs; each one had they're under arms shaved smooth. Now in any normal situation you'd think to yourselves all of these beauties would be squirming and thrashing about, right? The answer to that would be most defiantly yes all of them would be. However, though all of these beauties were still hypnotically entranced; but also in addition to this each of them could be seen wearing blindfolds over their eyes. With the exception of the Mellon sister who were here purely for their captures amusement. Connie Braxton, and Maxine Augustine on the other hand were most defiantly here for their information regarding their father's businesses. Sitting now in front of his victim's bare feet; their mysterious captor grins upon the completion, and satisfactory work thus far of his attendant's performance. As he next silently signals them next to inject the beauties with his special serum. His grin becomes much wider as they begin doing just that into their right arms. The rooms silence could be heard next being broken by the sounds of multiple fingers being snapped by the attendants close to the lovely victim's ears. Awakening to the horror and realization to what was going on. Screams of desperation and wanting to be released could be heard from each of the ladies as they struggled against their bonds to escape. Snickering amongst themselves however their captor's men just watched in amusement. As each lady attempts to either pull their arms down or for that matter pull their feet back only met with discouraging results from each of them.

Motioning his attendants next down to where the mysterious captor was standing in front of the beauties feet; he watches as they do just that taking their place in front of a particular pair.

"Ladies, Ladies, Ladies, as much as it's been fun listening to your screaming for help, or for that matter watching you struggling to get your arms and feet free. I must tell you it's sadly useless to even try; because as my slave's freedom for all of you is just a memory now."

Naturally expecting some kind of response to be forth coming the mysterious captor stands there with his arms folded just waiting patiently. Having carefully processed what each beauty thought they heard into each of their minds; they next decided to respond back in each of their unique way.

"Vickie, Vickie, tell this fucking idiot were not his slaves; I'm much too young to be anyone's slave." Tori exclaimed loudly with tears in her eyes struggling to look in her sister's direction,

"Listen to me Tori, calm down it'll be all right you're not going to be anyone's slave none of us are." Screams of confirmation could be heard next throughout the room from the others in agreement with Vickie.

Though it truly warmed the cockles of his heart to see the sisters trying to re-assure one another everything was going to be all right; but sadly, it wouldn't be.

"That's right Vickie, you tell this fucking idiot were not going to be anyone's slave that's right. Tori; your sister's correct were going to get out of here!"

Maxine exclaimed loudly followed lastly by Connie Braxton's response.

"Hey psycho you hear that! where ever you are? We're not afraid of you, so LET US GO NOW!" Silently laughing to himself their mysterious captor couldn't help but be impressed with these slaves, and all their piss and vinegar.

"Well now, I most defiantly have to applaud all of you. Bravo for your assertiveness given the predicament you are in, but far be it for me to squelch the illusions you have of being released anytime soon, because sadly that isn't going to happen." Never one to give into the emotions of his slaves and their demands upon him he knew that couldn't happen.

So now their mysterious captor silently motions two of the attendants to begin demonstrating to the others that wanting to be freed was not an option.

In any normal situation, anyone being given the opportunity to see what was happen to them could very well fake being ticklish and merely giggle to their captor in response. But tragically in this case believe me it's ten times worse; because you see while Connie and Maxine were forced to listen painfully as it was for them.

Victoria and Tori just couldn't imagine it getting any worse for them as their captor's attendants could be seen lightly tickling the feet of both sisters.

Naturally the table could be felt shaking as both sisters squirmed and thrashed about wildly. As each felt the different tools being applied to their high arched feet resulting at times with hysterical screams of laughter omitting from each of them.

Holding up his hand some forty minutes later immediately halting his attendants from commencing any further with the demonstration. As Victoria and Tori could be seen clearly gasping for breath at the same time mouthing deliriously "No More, No More."

"Aww, what's wrong ladies didn't you have fun?" Watching their heads frantically shaking no from side to side obviously meant they had in the eyes of the demented captor.

"Well congratulations ladies; being school girls like you are, at least now you can never say you're not majoring in something together." But rather being the only one laughing at his joke of his. He next motions his attendants to from before to use their fingers to tickle the toes of Victoria and Tori for a few seconds.

"You see ladies I can be humorous when I put my mind to it." He exclaims as he holds his hand up for the two attendants to stop. But while Tori and Victoria were trying their best to regain their individual composure. The mysterious captor motions the two other attendants up to help Maxine and Connie to lose theirs.

Poised with feathers the newest attendants slowly use them upon the helpless feet of Connie and Maxine. Impressed greatly with the same reaction he had seen with the Mellon Sisters earlier.

Left the mysterious captor grinning with joy even more seeing Maxine and Connie thrashing their bodies about the same way. Whispering to the other attendants within minutes the room was filled with laughter and sensual moaning combined.

As Maxine and Connie were being slowly tickled upon their feet laughing hysterically and thrashing about wildly. Tori and Victoria however were having their feet slowly licked and their toes sucked.

CHAPTER TWO

Several hours passed much to our amazement, as we could be seen lounging inside of the hammock just holding one another in our arms.

The barbecued meal prepared by my wife earlier was another stellar effort on her part. But I personally had to admit her appetizer was simply marvelous as well.

Lori's head could be seen resting itself upon my chest; watching her lifting it slightly to look into my eyes; I alertly listened as she exclaimed next.

"Penny for your thoughts?" Smiling back my hands gently rubbed her back caressing it lightly. "Oh, I was just thinking about how much I love you that's all baby." I said to her as my lips leaned into kiss her passionately.

"That's really sweet of you to say that honey; I love you to, but come on I can tell something's bothering you. I mean you seem so occupied with something you're thinking about, so talk to me about it; tell me about it; who knows it just might help?" I knew even if I was to tell her it's nothing to be concerned with; believe me she'd want to help anyway regardless, and I did love her for that.

"Alright baby, I'll tell you what's bothering me maybe your right just might help having you listen." Carefully helping her off the hammock I to found myself getting off; As I watched her sitting down at the poolside table I joined her shortly after retrieving my brief case.

Once I had; I began explaining everything to her about the meeting earlier. To my investigating Miss Davis's car, to the two pieces of evidence I discovered in there.

Not to mention my visions I experienced not only in her apartment; but in my car driving home tonight. I even for the first time opened to show Lori-Ann the articles in the large manila envelope. Sitting there watching her trying to process it all.

It suddenly occurred to her just what a mystery I was indeed up against.

"Wow, now I can see why your involved with your thoughts,"

"Yep; that's the case so far in a nutshell, but even though I can't make sense of the evidence yet; I did discover one thing today?"

"What's that honey?"

"My brother Elvis proposed marriage to this young lady, and she said yes on New Year's Eve in Times Square."

"So, your brothers engaged; What did you see that in one of your visions?"

"Ah huh, in my car coming home earlier; I pulled off to the side of the road in the breakdown lane; looked at the picture of them together in New York City; and bam it hit me showed him proposing to her."

"Well that's great, isn't it?"

"Oh yeah, sure it's great; my only worry now is finding Elvis before he hears it from someone else that's all and loses it all together." Carefully Lori-Ann watched my new look of concern upon my face about my own brother.

And just how indeed he is going to react hearing it from someone other than me.

So, while Lori and I pondered these things I had just said about the case. Our telephone rang suddenly causing us both to jump a little.

Laughing at one another with our hands on our chests; I then found myself getting up to answer it. "Hello Eddie James speaking can I help you?" Listening on the other end I could hear some papers shuffling around as I next heard.

"Hello Eddie, Listen I'm sorry as all hell to do this, but I'm going to need you back here at police headquarters." Upon hanging up my head fell swiftly to my chest over this news, but really what could I have done.

"I hate like hell to have to do this sweetie, but I have to go back to police headquarters for a briefing or something…ERG I don't want to go but I have too." Clearly Lori-Ann could see I had to go, but in her creative way of hastening my return she merely exclaimed to me.

"Go if you have to honey, I Understand, but just don't be surprised when you come home I might just have a little something for you tonight." It now wouldn't be until walking past me that I caught her winking her eye towards me as she continued slowly entering the house.

Having showered and dressed I was officially out of the house by 8:05P.M. and ready to rock. Though I had to admit that really wasn't my personal best time considering I spent the last ten minutes kissing my wife passionately still for me it was a taste of much more to come later.

Knowing when to drive into Boston; and when not to drive in was text book basic for surviving your big city experience.

You don't want to drive in the early morning hours between 6 & 9am and you most defiantly want to be out by 3:00PM. Because take it from me; people have a tendency to get super impatient with others after 4:00PM.

Who knows maybe my wife did me a favor in delaying my departure from the house by ten minutes.

In any event I certainly wasn't complaining when I was kissing her.

Just pulling into the precinct parking lot a little past 8:30pm most definitely was a personal best for me.

I saw myself parking next to a silver/black GMC flatbed truck belonging to my cousin. As a smile could be seen upon my face, I thought reflectively about the really cool times we spent going fishing together in that truck.

My cousins full name was Robert Joseph James but even though people in Washington referred to him as Robert; we still called him B.J.

Having watched him his senior year playing football I had a feeling even back then his toughness as a nose tackle was merely a prelude to better things to come for him.

Immediately after graduating high school; he found himself being accepted to Boston Collage on a football scholarship so he went there.

Burying himself in criminal law and criminal justice books most of the time he settled into his collegiate carrier as an academic student.

Where four years later he graduated in the spring of 1986 where he took his education to Washington and the F.B.I. who he still works for today.

It took me several minutes before I re-entered Uncle Jesse's office once again.

After shaking his hand then I turned to see B.J. setting up a projector for his briefing. "Hey Cuz, How's the bureau been treating you?"

"Hey Eddie, Hi, the bureau? They've been treating me all right I guess I mean up until this latest case they assigned me to."

"Oh yeah what one?"

"Are you kidding me the one that's had this country literally handcuffed for two and half years. That's the one they assigned me to; and to tell you the truth between you and me I'm stumped."

"Well no disrespect to you cuz, but I'm happy as shit you being on board on this one, because the evidence I've uncovered so far is kicking my ass severely."

"Really you to huh, hey congrats by the way my dad told me you were hired to locate this lady Brenda Davis for her Father."

"Thanks, cuz, yeah he hired me." It wouldn't be until placing some folders out upon the table before B.J. was ready to begin his presentation

"All right Gentlemen if you'll take your seats now I believe I'm just about ready to start." Watching Uncle Jesse taken his usual seat at the head of the table

I took mine just to his right; as B.J. Began.

"I'd like to call your attention to this first young lady her name is Victoria Mellon, she's a 19yr old college freshman who enrolled at Florida State University when she was abducted along with her 17yr old sister Tori five miles away from the campus." I briefly glanced at Victoria's folder until B.J. was prepared to speak once more.

"This young lady is Maxine Augustine a fiery red head as you can see. She is 20yrs old according to my sources she is a telemarketer by day, and a party girl at night. Apparently, she went to the beach during the week; rented a pedal boat then mysteriously disappeared in the ocean somewhere." Briefly glancing at her folder.

"This third young lady is 19yr old Connie Braxton she as you can see here is an Afro-American. She is a medical intern.

At U-Mass who on her day off was heading to the beach when she mysteriously disappeared at a traffic light. Witnesses who stepped forward reported she left her car in the first lane to climb into a second vehicle leaving her car there to drive off with the occupants of the second vehicle."

It seemed to me that these were random as I glanced at Connie's folder.

"Last but certainly not meant to be least is Victoria's younger sister Tori Mellon she is a 17yrs old high school student who is about to enter her senior year. When like I said earlier she disappeared together with her sister five miles away from the Florida State campus."

After turning back on the lights, I next could be seen gathering up the folders then placing them into my brief case.

"Talk about some weird shit huh cuz; five ladies in two days you'd think this wacko was starting a harem or something?"

"Dose sound weird don't it; hey answer a question for me if you could?" "Shoot."

"Just what did their fathers do for work? I'm just curious."

"Good question cuz." Double checking his records B.J. next exclaimed.

"Alright, says here that Miss Braxton's father is get this a Ugandan Diplomat, Miss Augustine's Father is a bank executive with a Chicago Bank with access to various accounts, and lastly the Mellon sister's father owns and operates his own construction company down in Florida."

It still didn't make sense here were three fathers each with diverse occupations whose daughters were taken for what reason?

It wouldn't be until checking my watch that I saw it was 9:45PM After saying goodnight to Uncle Jesse; I said to B.J. that I'd be giving him a call tomorrow morning to get together and go over the evidence we had. Maybe our two heads together just could spark something in a direction we could go with this.

According to the files I did scan B.J. was right all of these ladies were quite diverse indeed. Two were students, one was a medical intern, and the other was a telemarketer. In addition to each of their fathers also being diverse as well. But the question that kept gnawing at me was what did they all have in common. It may have been one thing being a private investigator focusing on a case like this; I really wanted to tag first time out of the bull pen.

But in all honesty, I just couldn't disappoint Lori-Ann with my over thinking of this present case I was on. The temperature was 72 with the wind light feeling the breeze thru my windows. A Seals and Croft song was playing on one of my classic rock stations I listened to. The cars passed by me on the highway as music could be heard from them within their own confines.

Two bikinis clad young ladies hung their pretty heads out of a car in front of me screaming they loved the summer time, and really who could blame them. My personal focus was on my lovely wife's little surprise once I arrived home once again.

There were times I'd be in the bathroom showering with shampoo in my eyes; she'd slip herself quietly in behind me; then wrap her slender arms around me pulling me back into her.

I felt her breasts upon the middle of my back. Another grin appeared upon my face as I thought of her listening to my radio. Tapping my foot to Otis Reading's "Sitting on the dock of the bay" Actually this was the first song Lori-Ann and I heard after our marriage back in Williamsburg to which we slow danced too.

Pulling into the driveway then getting out of my car I looked over at my Harley parked in front of my 1979 Oldsmobile Cutlass. Thinking to myself that car could screw off the line.

Opening the front door, I smelled a honeysuckle scent; my eyes noticed candles lit leading upstairs; then noticed red hearts cut out of red silk paper going up the stairs too.

Smiling; once more listening I heard "sitting on the dock of the bay" by Ottis Reading playing as my feet were careful walking by the candles up the stairs; they were small in clear glass holders. The silk hearts stopped at our bed room door.

Her smile lit up the room walking in I closed the door. Seeing completely different crystal holders throughout they burned brightly in a reddish hugh.

Lori-Ann was dressed in her see thru nighty; as I approached the bed. I noticed a bucket of ice and a bottle of Champaign chilling in the gold colored bucket with two crystal glasses beside her; in a medium sized bowel, also beside her were freshly cut strawberries.

"Looks like you were busy while I was gone sweetheart."

"Just a little bit baby; thought you might like my surprise I set out here for us."

"Yes, very much so sweetheart I am impressed as I walked in candles leading up here, the silk red rose hearts to on the floor as well, and coming in here seeing these taller candle holders what's not to like?"

Smiling watching me leaning into her she reaches back getting a fresh cut strawberry from the bowel offering it to me as I laid beside her. Biting it gently I kissed her fingers smiling back at her reaching over to get one offering it to her which she giggly accepted biting it gently kissing my fingers too.

Lying beside Lori we continued gently feeding each other from the medium sized bowel of strawberries; then kissing each other playing with each other's tongues.

Sliding my finger along her left arm it catches the strap gently pulling it down her off her shoulder.

Grinning it lets out a pleasant surprise pop out before me.

"Ahem aren't the strawberries enough for you to eat sweetheart?"

"Actually, not when I have as beautiful as a main course of you to feast upon darling."

Smiling leaning into each our tongues capture the others listening hearing her soft moans as my right finger recaptures the strap of her right shoulder pulling down the strap.

It didn't take long for me to unbutton my shirt before Lori dropped herself down to start kissing my upper chest then my breast nipples sucking upon them gently.

While she keeps on kissing and sucking my chest nipples watching I see her aggressively removing her nighty throwing upon the floor.

Taking off my jeans continuing to watch her Lori looks up at me with her eyes playfully.

Pulling me hard down upon her our bodies wrap themselves within each other; as our kisses turn more passionately.

Our hands move caressing the other's body each bringing the other much more into a heated desire for the other; as our legs caress the others.

Our bodies immediately felt our inner flame of burning passion building to a great crow Shendo as we thrashed about wildly rolling the other upon the other; again, and again.

Across town however a very tired and burned out Stacy McKenna was just walking out, and across the parking lot toward her car. Having volunteered to stay and fill out reports may not have been on her top ten things to do list tonight; she knew it still needed to be done never the less.

But thinking about it in the long run being the daughter of the bureau director did have its perks. Stacy stands 6'3" and weighs 115lbs with long straight light brown hair; and hazel eyes. Tonight, she decided to wear a very short black skirt with no nylons on; and a white button downed short sleeve blouse; and her choice of footwear were flip flops. Always hating to wear shoes as a rule especially in the summertime Stacy could always be seen driving bare foot almost anywhere she traveled. Immediately after slipping her feet out of her flip flops: Stacy next could be seen in frustration having to bend over to pick up her car keys she accidentally dropped. Even though her immediate thoughts may have been to be inside of her car and seeing herself driving homeward. Sadly, however that wouldn't be happening for her tonight. Because it wouldn't be until standing back up that her eyes were hit with 2 green colored beams of light. Instantly placing Miss Stacy McKenna into a very deep hypnotic trance. Carefully watching; she immediately drops her things right beside her feet; just as a mysterious black van pulls itself up directly behind her. While the driver remained behind the wheel watching Stacy getting inside of it. His partner however could be seen outside placing Miss McKenna's things into the back seat of her car; including the very clothes she was wearing.

Within minutes after closing the side door of the van the two men could be seen driving away with their newest and very naked objective having been achieved. If getting up to go to the bathroom wasn't bad enough; try getting up to a ringing telephone at 4:00AM.

"Hello"

"Eddie, Hey Cuz, hate to wake you but we had another abduction here at F.B.I. Headquarters, but I think we caught a break, how soon can you get here?

"What, what time is it B.J.?"

"Sorry to say it's 4:00AM"

"Ah give me forty-five minutes or so, I'll be there, hey by the way have some coffee ready for me huh? I think I'm going to need it, extra-large and regular dude."

"Gotcha covered cuz, just get here when you can?"

It wouldn't be until getting into the bathroom; before I realized the importance of my cousin's call. The last time I use to get up at 4am was to start jogging in preparation for a martial arts tournament

where I had to defend my latest title.

The time was ten minutes before five in the morning before I could be seen driving into the parking lot of F.B.I. headquarters.

From the looks of things, I suddenly realized I wasn't at the policeman's ball.

It now wouldn't be until opening my car door before Uncle Jesse, B.J. and another gentleman I didn't know walked up to my car.

Handing me a coffee I thanked B.J. for not forgetting it, and continued sitting there sipping it as I next heard.

"Commissioner, I'd like an explanation please, as to why no one is investigating what happened here yet, and further more why my agent here gave this man a large coffee upon his coming here, WHO IS THIS MAN!"

Watching B.J. shaking his head, he knew just how I was going to react, so he didn't stop me.

"Ah First Off Porky, why don't you calm down and let me wake up first before you start demanding useless explanations; Second your agent here happens to be my cousin; and he shouldn't have to jump through hopes for the likes of you, so back off. And third he hasn't started this investigation yet because he called me and was waiting for me to get here. Oh, and by the way in case you were still wondering; I asked him before to get me one of these; and lastly so you know; my names Eddie James, and yes if your still stunned I am a Private Investigator…. Good Morning."

"Wow dude, I can't believe you did that; do you know who that was?"

"Doesn't matter cuz, but listen on the phone earlier you mentioned something about catching a break, what did you mean when you said that?" I asked as we were walking toward Miss McKenna's car.

"Oh yeah, well our security camera caught something weird on video tape that's all."

But before either of us could go see exactly what was on that surveillance tape; I suddenly stopped myself closing my eyes then seeing the very first images passing before me.

Figuring Uncle Jesse may have told him B.J. didn't try to touch me in anyway as he kept watching me. *The first image was of a young lady wearing a black mini-skirt, a white short sleeve blouse, and flip flops on her feet. The second image was of her standing barefoot bending down to pick up her keys that she apparently dropped.*

My ability couldn't just let me see what happened next however it did flash a license plate number that simply read: X-K-A-BAR.

Shaken my head upon awakening I next could be seen Placing my hand upon her car when it quickly happened once more for some unknown reason.

In this next image, it just showed someone dressed in black placing what looked like her things into her car then quickly leaving.

Leaning myself up against her car next trying to recompose myself after my sixth sense double whammed me.

Needless to say, caught B.J. completely off guard to what was happening.

Kneeling down next with my back against the driver's side door watching Uncle Jesse glancing over to us.

He next see's B.J. kneeling down in front of me perplexed of what to do next.

"Da" Grabbing his arm quickly he watches me exclaiming next.

"B.J. Go over and get your father but don't call out like that to draw further attention upon me; Jesus dude if other people find out I have this ability they'll be calling me wanting to know all sorts of things you got it?" I could feel his look of almost making a mistake, as he slowly stood up still watching me. "Hey Cuz go, don't worry about me I'm all right this will pass trust me it always does." Continuing to watch me out of the corner of his right eye pulling his father aside to speak to him; the two of them next could be seen walking back towards me.

"Eddie, are you all right B.J. tells me you saw something?" Nodding my head before exclaiming. "Yeah, Uncle Jesse you could say I got hit with a double whammy of sorts, but before I go telling you about it, do either of you have a pen and a note pad?"

It wouldn't be until being handed these items that they continued watching me jotting something down. Ripping it off the pad I next hand it to my cousin.

"Take that plate number there; and run it through the D.M.V. then let me know what you come up with?" It wouldn't be until seeing Uncle Jesse nodding his head that B.J. next started walking away from us to run that plate number.

"Listen Eddic, are you sure your all right?" Catching the look of concern on his face was appreciative but in reality, it didn't explain to me my double whammy of visions I had experienced several minutes ago.

"Yes, Uncle Jesse thank you, I'm fine though you know me when these things hit me."

"Sure, I do indeed, but come on Eddie tell me what happened; what did you see?" Pulling him away from the car I next exclaimed.

"All right Uncle Jesse here goes the first thing I saw was a lady coming out this building she had long brown hair, and she was wearing a white short sleeve blouse, flip slops on her feet, not to mention she has on a black mini-skirt. She looked to be about 6'3" tall, and couldn't have weighed more than 115lbs. Unfortunately, I wasn't able to see what happened to her?"

"I see, well what about that license plate number you wrote down and gave to your cousin to run for you; what's that about?"

"Oh, sorry Uncle Jesse; the license plate number's what I'd seen last before these images faded from my sight; so, I jotted it down for B.J. to try and run at the D.M.V."

Seeing him now with his arms folded starring at the ground next I could hear him exclaim.

"So that explains why Mr. McKenna; Porky to you Eddie was so upset earlier when you arrived here; it would also explain his being here in the first place; but my only question is why?

Because that young lady you described earlier is none other than his daughter Stacy."

My uncle was right it didn't make sense for him being here; sure, he may have been the director of the F.B.I.

And yes, he was the father of the abducted lady; but come on there are procedures; and protocols which his men knew. And besides his being here was an additional distraction for his men to always look over their shoulder before doing anything connected to the case.

I next could be seen walking beside my Uncle; as we went to checkout that surveillance tape together.

Miles away however Stacy McKenna was at this moment being carefully evaluated for a completely different carrier choice in a field she'd soon be referring to as human slavery.

The room she found herself being guided into was an extremely larger sized throne room of sorts.

With super smooth high polished wooden floors to walk upon; and pillars to gaze at throughout.

Positioned laying spread eagle on the floor Stacy sadly could be seen their nude with a leather hood placed over her head in between four of the pillars.

Having already been injected with a syringe of the mysterious captor's serum upon her arriving there.

The daughter of the F.B.I. director continues waiting for whoever had her to reveal themselves. However, within minutes listening she hears the snaps of fingers that instantly awakens her to the horror she was about to face.

"God where the hell am I?"

"Why am I laying on the floor of all places; and Urg why can't I get up for that matter?" "Huh, What the. No, I'm naked who the hell did this me?"

Even though she had legitimate questions they paled into comparison to what she was about to go through now.

Suddenly from the silence of the room Stacy awoken to find herself in.

Came next the thunderous eruption of laughter springing forth out of her.

As she felt the softest fingers of whoever had her; tickling Stacy's body in varies areas with Maxine Augustine using her soft fingers in her armpits as well as her rib cages.

Connie Braxton meanwhile was laying on her stomach with her bare-feet lifted behind her. Using not only her soft fingers; but her talented tongue as well to tease and torture Stacy's feet and toes.

Resulting in Stacy being absolutely helpless before them.

CHAPTER THREE

CHAPTER THREE

Meanwhile back in Boston we gathered at Police Headquarters although nothing had been uncovered by the lab boys in and around the parking lot; or for that matter around Miss McKenna's car.

The F.B.I. surveillance tape however did manage to undercover another additional piece of this bizarre mystery.

Having seen the two green beams of light being cast into the eyes of Miss McKenna did suggest to us simply; that whoever was responsible for these missing women were controlling them with some sort of hypnotic device resulting in anyone seeing them getting into some kind of vehicle.

Though Uncle Jesse and B.J. were convinced my theory was sound enough to make sense of; still there was that intangible thing called proof.

We still needed that to convince anyone else; or especially a district attorney that my theory wasn't lame.

"All right, so we have this tape showing something happening to Miss McKenna that caused her to get into the van; but come on Eddie if I were to bring this to the attention of the D.A. He'd laugh at me, oh after that he'd throw me out of his office on my head."

"Wouldn't want that to happen, but OK. Maybe we do need more solid proof before approaching anyone; so, let's shift gears then what if anything did you find out about that license plate number I gave you earlier?"

"Well," the individual whose plate number you gave me doesn't exist according to my source at the R.M.V. He's dead I had him check and re-check their information to before I came back here."

"Great, well did this source of yours have a name of this person at least?" "Ah huh my source says his name was Maxwell Escobar." "His file says anything about what he was convicted for?"

"Oh yeah, extortion, assault and battery, but the biggie he was convicted for was first degree murder." "Who'd he kill?"

"That's the strange part, no on I spoke with knows, or if they do there not tell me. My guess if I were to make one, would be he killed a local business man who refused to pay him."

"Hmm, that dose sound strange you'd think his conviction would be on file somewhere, or someone would've known who he killed?"

"Sorry cuz, as good as an agent as I am even I couldn't dig up that info?"

Whoever this Escobar guy was certainly was fortunate to have his conviction records dying with him my question naturally of course was why?

Checking my watch shortly after leaving police headquarters to see it was a little past 11:30a.m.

Strongly suggested I hadn't eaten since our barbecue last night.

Don't get me wrong the coffee I did have this morning was great and it naturally helped me to wake up all right; a little before five in the morning.

But sadly, it didn't help my stomach any further from growling.

So, pulling off the main road behind The Black Dragon Restaurant I next could be seen parking beside an all to recognizable white colored Lambo.

Admiring his car for a moment my mind slipped itself back into nostalgia.

I first met him walking home from school one day; mind you I never went out of my way looking for trouble, but seeing what I saw this one day with 3 guys pushing him around for no apparent reason; I just couldn't just walk by without doing something.

So, after tripping the three of them hard on their ass's they just picked themselves up and walked away without further incident.

Seeing him pick up his book, I helped him out picking up the last two handing them to him. "Thank you for the assist with those guys, I really didn't know why they were harassing me for?" "You're welcome my pleasure; and my guess as to why they harassed you is pretty evident two of the boys are rich, and spoiled by their father. I've seen their types before praying on those who couldn't defend themselves against them. But are you OK. they didn't hurt you, did they?"

"No, I'm not hurt at least not physically well maybe just my pride is."

The boy who stood before was shy and reserved but I could sense he would have loved to leg sweep those fools like I did.

"My names Eddie, Eddie James" Looking to me surprised shaking hands.

"My names Michael, Michael Stanton, wow the kids at school aren't going to believe I actually know you; I seen you in an exhibition demonstration once last month in gym you got some amazing moves."

"Thanks Michael, lot of practice to perfect those moves over the years." Smiling at one another we each went our separate ways after that talk.

I went back home grabbed something to eat, and did my homework then around seven o'clock I went for my nightly run.

When I stopped at a brownstone with police cars and an ambulance there; the area had yellow caution police tape around the perimeter.

As I made my way closer to it I saw a patrolman bringing out Michael Stanton the kid I met earlier out in handcuffs escorting him to a marked cruiser.

"Uncle Jesse?" Watching him looking over at me he signals one of the officer's in front of me to let me through.

"Did you eat dinner and do your homework?"

"Yeah just out taking my run when I saw this what; what happened here?"

"Triple murder; Mother, Father And younger sister from the looks of it, call came into the station person was unknown who called. But said they heard gun shots coming from this address, so a black/white responded looked in a window saw the 3 bodies called for backup and this is what they found."

"Where was Michael, the kid they brought out?"

"Oh, he was lying in bed had the gun in his hand when we woke him up started freaking out when he saw the gun in his hand reflex he threw the gun across his bedroom."

As I listened something smelled off to me my impression upon meeting him earlier suggested this kid didn't have an aggressive bone in his body.

Leaving the crime scene, I continued my run thinking to myself to get to the bottom of this the next day.

Michael Stanton from what I saw of him was a reserved shy quiet kid, or so he seemed. According to certain teachers I spoke to he was a very bright and diligent student in class, and was according to the basketball coach a very good basketball player when he was on the court.

So, with all that going for him why risk doing what he did to his family it still didn't add up in my mind.

After school, instead of going straight home I walked to police headquarters to talk with Uncle Jesse.

I began explaining to him that I started doing some digging around school about Michael, at which all my Uncle could do was smile and nod his head.

Uncle Jesse knew me, and 99% of the time believed in my opinions concerning anyone I thought was innocent.

"So, see you've taken an interest in this Eddie?"

'Yes, Uncle Jesse and please it's no disrespect to you or your other officers, but I have this gut feeling this kid's been set up for this."

"Have that feeling to myself, but I kind of need to go with the process here."

"Oh of course Uncle Jesse I understand where you're coming from, but do you think I could talk with him." Watching him smiling he gabs his keys as I follow him walking out of an office room.

"Hi Michael, how they treating you?"

"Not bad thank you, surprised as hell you'd be here though?" "Don't be this is my Uncle Jesse here."

"Nice to meet you Michael, sorry for the handcuffs."

"It's OK suppose your just doing your job and all."

Smiling Uncle Jesse just nods his head next before exclaiming.

"I know you've told your story already to the detectives, but could you tell my nephew it now?'

"Sure, well like I told the detectives before I had just finished my snack and was sitting on my bed about to start my homework when I heard a knock at my door, so I went to answer it to see it was one of the boys before who was harassing me earlier when we first met Eddie."

Nodding my head to Michael…. "Do you remember who it was?"

"Yeah, this Theo Simpson kid, he said he came to apologize for his part in that mess before, and even bought me an orange juice as a piece offering to show he had no grudge against me."

"I see, and what happened next after that?"

"We talked for a few minutes then he left after I finished drinking the o.j. then went back to doing my homework then after I crashed on my bed."

"You feel asleep?"

"Yeah was suddenly tired, then next thing I know I wake up holding some gun in my left hand it freaked me out; that's when the police came into my bedroom seeing it in my hand."

"Hmm, dose seem strange." It wouldn't be until telling him to hang in there before Uncle Jesse and I left him.

"Something tells me your thinking the same thing I am Eddie?"

"Only if you're thinking that this smells of a set-up then yea your thinking the same as me alright." Uncle Jesse always said to me when you feel in your gut something is wrong go with your instincts because your instincts will never lie to you on what your guts telling you. And mine surprisingly was pointing to three possible suspects Scott Wilson, Randy Wilson, and Theo Simpson.

They were the three who were harassing Michael the day we met.

While I did my normal thing going to classes I started asking around about the three of them.

I heard that the Wilson boys always had their classes together, and while they were there they always acted obnoxious, and arrogant. Shaking my head not surprised at the teachers and students I did talk to about them walking away I always thought to myself (Yep like my instincts always told me about these two they were rich boys who could get away with everything only because they were rich.)

Then when I asked about Theo Simpson it wasn't any surprise there I heard he was reserved and a lot of times easily coerced into doing things he normally wouldn't think of doing on his own then I heard a few people saying that the Wilson boys were the one's pushing him to do those certain things.

Now my main focus quickly switched to following and observing Theo Simpson figuring he's be the one who'd crack out of all of them.

One day as I was waiting for a class to begin when I overheard a conversation next to me between Theo Simpson and Randy Wilson.

"I can't do this Randy this is killing me…I can't sleep I'm having nightmares about."

"Shut up you Lil; just don't blow this for my brother and me and we'll get away with it, just keep yourself together." Randy walked aggressively passed me as he left Theo standing there.

After school, I walked straight to police headquarters and met with Uncle Jesse. Bringing him up to speed on what I found out while at school, he had a black/white bring Theo Simpson in.

I Stood watching as Theo just sat there in the interrogation room unsure as to why he was there tapping his finger nervously.

"Good afternoon Theo; I'm sergeant James thank you for coming in to see us today I'm sorry can I call you Theo?"

"Sure; ahh did I do something wrong, because I've never been in a place like this?"

"No, you didn't do anything wrong; we just need to ask you some questions regarding that Stanton Murders."

"You did hear about that didn't you someone shooting Mr. and Mrs. Stanton and their 6yr old daughter Rachel. We got a phone tip from a caller they saw someone matching your description was walking around their brownstone apartment building is that true?"

Before he could answer a female officer could be seen interrupting by sticking her head in the room.

"Excuse me sergeant but there's a telephone call for you." Nodding his head to her Uncle Jesse gets up but not before placing in front of Theo the photographs of Mr., &Mrs. Stanton and their daughter Rachel for Theo to stare at.

"Stay here Theo and take a good look at these photo's maybe something will come to you; I'll be right back after taking care of this phone call." Leaving him their Uncle Jesse joined me in the room adjoining to watch Theo with me.

"How did I do in there Eddie?"

"Very convincing Uncle Jesse; now let's watch and see if my theory about him cracking pains out." Minutes passed before we witnessed Theo pushing the picture off the table in front of him.

"Oh God; I can't, I can't do this…. this is killing me…I can't sleep at night.

Arrrrg…. Why did I listen to Scott and Randy…? I swear God they were the ones who killed Mr. and Mrs. Stanton…. then they tossed that blasted gun then yelled at me to shoot that innocent lil' girl…. God Forgive me please I can't take it anymore all I see when I close my eyes is that lil' girl's face." Together Uncle Jesse and I nodded our heads listening to Theo Simpson confessing from the adjoining room as we watched him thru the two-way mirror.

Shortly however we re-entered that interrogation room while Uncle Jesse and I stood and watched as Theo Simpson wrote out his statement of what really happened.

Uncle Jesse after which sent out a black/white to bring in the Wilson boys, Michael Stanton was brought up before he could get a chance to even see the Wilson boys coming into the station.

When Scott and Randy were brought in they were escorted to central booking and processing.

The officer who brought Michael in took his hand cuffs of him, then left us.

"Eddie, What, what's going on?""

"Your free Michael, the guilty were caught for your family's murders." "Huh? Who How?"

"I overheard Theo Simpson at school just outside of one of my classes talking with Randy Wilson about not being able to do it; he said he had nightmares to Randy about what happened. So, I had a theory regarding Theo Simpson being a week link to what the Wilson Boys did.

So, we had him brought in and he cracked after we showed him pictures of your Mother, Father, and little sister." Looking at me with a tear flowing down his cheek. He gave me a big hug in gratitude for what I did in clearing him of these charges against him.

Shaking my head coming out of that I smiled to myself. Naturally it wouldn't be immediately that I'd see him; but I quickly sensed he was there just watching and waiting for his opportunity to present himself.

So, after I placed my breakfast order with Sue in the kitchen; I took my seat at the counter. Having been told I looked like hell slightly improved my mood considerably compared to what it was before.

But now as I continued sitting there with my breakfast order in. I next turned my thoughts to coffee with a very huge emphasis on java, at this point while I sat and waited.

"Good morning Eddie." Danny exclaimed watching him placing a few menus away in their holders.

"Good morning Danny, say you got a minute to spare?" Watching him walking over to me he then says back.

"Sure, Eddie what's up?" After which I then pull out of my pocket a copy of that license plate number for him to keep.

"Danny do you think you can show this around to your contacts and try to see if they know about where it came from.

I already had B.J. check with the D.M.V. but he came up with nothing in the way of information on it." Carefully placing it away he next says back.

"It would be my pleasure Eddie consider it done, oh by the way there's some guy here who'd like to see you on the case you're working on.

He told me he just arrived from Florida, says he's working on the same case too. I don't know though maybe he just wants to meet you and compare crib notes."

Shifting his eyes slightly to the right I noticed his smile getting wider, as he gestures his head in that direction.

Turning around I caught sight of the very individual he was making reference too.

Smiling myself getting up off my seat. Danny continues watching as this individual and I embrace one another in a mutual hug of friendship.

In a time, long ago before this AIDS thing took hold of everyone there once was a practice performed between kids where they'd cut each other enough to mix each other's blood in a symbolic ritual making themselves blood brothers.

And his name is simply Snake, and as weird as it may sound; he is mine.

Standing 7ft tall in height, and yes if you're wondering he could've been a basketball player if tragedy hadn't struck killing his family in a senseless act of violence where that dream in itself was buried along with his true identity.

Moving from the counter to a nearby table Snake and I could be seen catching up on old times before we starting to talk shop.

"I see you still carry the scare upon your hand as I do?" Smiling we each looked at the scares upon or right hands.

"Yes, it's a day I always reflect upon in great memory my friend." Smiling back at me we each took a sip of our coffee's.

"Danny mentioned to me your working on the same case as me, congratulations Who hired you?" I exclaimed watching him stirring with his spoon.

"Thanks yeah I was hired by this guy down there to locate his missing daughters. Have you heard of a guy named Theo Mellon he owns Mellon Construction in Fort Lauderdale he's the one who hired me?"

Nodding my head towards him I watched him drinking his coffee as I replied back.

"Name dose sound familure, doesn't he have two daughters one a senior in high school, oh about 17yrs old, and another daughter who's about to begin collage this fall at Florida State University?" Taken in by my street savvy of just who he was actually referring to Snake could be heard next exclaiming.

"Very good Eddie, I'm impressed with your knowledge of just who I was hired to locate." Not meaning to after placing my hands together I then closed my eyes I half bowed to him in another symbolic gesture.

It had taken several minutes before we once again could be seen recomposing each other, but before we had a chance to resume our conversation a very distraught Sue Chang appeared in the kitchen doorway.

"Eddie, the police are at your house something's happened to your wife."

All we could do, as we made it out of there was pray, pray that no one got in either of our way as we left. "Tell me something can you still drive fast?"

Nodding his head toward me all I can remember saying to him next as we got into his car was. "FLOOR IT!"

Listening to hear Snake's tires squeal there in the parking lot we next within minutes could be seen shooting out back into traffic once more.

Having been around fast cars most of my life Snake's driving didn't bother me much. But I had to admit being in a car that could do 120 miles an hour did for all intents and purposes give me a rush to say the least.

It took us less than forty-five minutes before we could be seen pulling into the driveway of my house. But once we had I was immediately barraged by reporters wanting to know my take on what was happening and how I was feeling.

Thinking to myself "Oh yeah like you give two shits huh?" Amazing as that may have been my personal thought at the time. I certainly couldn't just blurt that out to them so I did what I've normally done with reporters in the past I didn't say a word.

While Snake canvased the rest of the house I went to look for my cousin and Uncle to find out what happened and what exactly was going on.

It wouldn't be until seeing them in the kitchen that I next looked past them toward my refrigerator to see the manila envelope hanging there behind them.

Someone once said shock when it hits you is like a quick punch to your gut it doubles you over and leaves you gasping for air.

Though I can't remember who quoted that little antidote but they were right, and I was. While I continued my struggle to make sense of this tragedy that has happened.

Lori-Ann however found herself miles away being lead down a strange corridor.

She could be seen like the others were completely naked with a leather collar around her neck clipped to that also was a leash.

Having already been introduced to the green lights Lori's eyes stared straight ahead, as she continued walking still being led by her attendant.

Standing just up ahead on the right rubbing his hands together is her mysterious host just watching his latest slave being lead over to him.

Seen grinning to himself; he next watches as the two enter the adjoined room next to him. "Congratulations Alexander yes you've done extremely well." Having seen his Master was indeed pleased with him meant the attendant would get a chance to shave her.

Watching Lori-Ann getting herself up upon the medical table with its back elevated; her mysterious captor watches Lori jump a little bit as her bare back meets the tables leather covering.

His attendant next could be viewed placing a leather strap around Lori-Ann's wrist tightly then raising them to a hook just above her head.

The attendant next is signaled to elevate Lori's legs so that her feet dangled in the air. So, With steel shackles attached to either side of a long pole her legs were lifted and her ankles were placed into these shackles.

It wouldn't be until stepping back to assess his handiwork before he could be seen lathering up his hands to start.

Slowly he could be seen lathering Lori's underarms, and her pleasure area, as well. Listening at times Alexander can hear Lori moaning softly toward him.

Standing just close enough to his attendant the mysterious captor nods his head in approval. As the attendant could be viewed working slowly and extra carefully.

Minutes later seeing his newest slave freshly shaven Lori's mysterious captor watches as the leather straps are taken down off the hook then removed from around her wrists. Then the shackles around Lori's ankles are next opened and her legs are lowered. Still grinning he watches as Lori gets down next off the table.

"Excellent job Alexander Bravo; ah now we can begin to interrogate her on what she knows about her husband's investigation."

Shortly after placing the clip from the leash back through Lori's collar she next could be seen being lead out of that previous room and walking back down the corridor.

Minutes passed as Lori and her attendant could be seen next re-entering another room.

This new room they found themselves in measured 24X24 with three lights dangling above their heads.

Also, just to either side of the room there stood two portable carts with drawers containing an assortment of special tools.

These tools he used ranged from feathers of every shape and size, to battery powered toothbrushes as well as manual ones, in one of the drawers he even had a few boxes of Q-tip swabs.

On the very tops of the carts there were small versions of riders crops with small leather squares to whack the soles of a victim's feet to stimulate them. Having her collar removed Lori-Ann's guided over to an extremely large table. The table measured 12X12 and was constructed on the tops of the 6X6 heavy duty construction columns. Just like in the throne room these also had been sanded smooth to the touch also stained to an equal mirrored finish. The tops of the table had a very plush carpeting with a thin wooden boarder that went around the edge of the table all the way around.

Lori's attendant kicked over a set of steps on wheels just in front of her. Slowly she began ascending to the very top of the table. After which her feet vanished into the plush carpeting. As she walked to the middle of it; laying her naked body down upon it

Positioning her arms and legs spread eagle before the attendant. Taking leather straps, he secured them around both her wrists and ankles holding her there firmly. The very last item placed over her head was a leather hood with a gold zipper around her mouth.

Arriving shortly after this was completed were four individuals. Two were beautiful ladies naked; escorted by two mysterious gentlemen who lead them both to assist in this special procedure that was to take place.

"All right Mr. X here she is; but are you sure you want this done?" Exclaimed the mysterious captor to his guest.

"Yes, Dammit Yes, I want this done for however long it takes to give me the information on what her husband is doing on this case, so that I can stay one step ahead of him. Or would you like his cousin and him to find you?" Asked his guest looking directly at him. "Good point Mr. X" Nodding his head they watched the two ladies standing next to them, as they walked to take their place in their separate positions.

Just behind Lori positioned to tickle her underarms and waist stood Victoria Mellon. Crawling on her hands and knees beneath Lori to tickle her also was Victoria's sister Tori. Flipping open a small five square section just in front of Lori-Ann's pleasure area Tori grinned devilishly as she waved her fingers up at her big sister through the hole. Upon their mysterious Master's signal Victoria now snapped her fingers twice into Lori's left ear, then twice in her right ear. Waking Lori to the horror she would be soon facing.

"Huh? What the hell? Where? Where am I? Why? Why am I naked?" Silently watching Lori-Ann struggling like she was whoever it was who had her expressed himself for the first time to her.

"So many questions Mrs. James but unfortunately for you they're without answers I'm not willing to share with you. But please by all means continue to struggle if you like; you'll quickly discover it's quite useless to escape." Listening, she hears his footsteps getting closer to her, then sensed his presents close to her.

"Oh, just you wait until I get out of here your sadistic son-of-a-bitch. Because if you never had your ass kicked by a woman before then try me out I'm sure of one thing you won't be sitting down for a while."

"But who knows maybe I'll just save that pleasure for my husband to do instead?" Listening Lori hears laughter coming from others unbeknownst to her.

Placing his fingers up to his lips signaling silence from the others the mysterious man speaks once again.

"Ah, Yes the mighty Eddie James; do tell me Mrs. James just how is his investigation going in trying to find me?" Hoping in his heart for the inevitable response he knows all too well he will be receiving from her.

"Oh, you must be dreaming if you think I'm going to betray my husband by telling you anything about him or his investigation." Lori exclaimed turning her head away from him in a huff.

"Tsk, Tsk, Tsk, that's really a shame you feel that way, well if there isn't anything I can do to change your mind Mrs. James; then at least let me try and put you into a much better mood seeing I might have upset you so."

Upon completing his speech to her; the man silently signals his slave to begin their torture upon Lori-Ann. Having injected Lori-Ann already with his special serum earlier causes her to erupt loudly in hysterical laughter As Victoria's fingers slowly circled the underarms of Lori then glides slower down her left and right rib cage. The feather lightly caressing Lori-Ann's pleasure area like it was from Tori added to the victim's hysterics. Not to mention a third girl near Lori's feet lightly caressing her soles with her slow finger then with her mouth starts sucking upon Lori-Ann's toes. Sadly, however just what Lori was experiencing here was merely the beginning of her torture.

Believe it or not the last time I felt helpless like this was when my parents died in that awful car explosion; but honestly what could I really do I was only 9 years old at the time.... But Now?

The scene at my house looked unreal to me as I watched everyone was moving in slow motion guys were going around gathering what if any finger prints or evidence was left behind and their voices sounded far off, distant, and half muffled.

Snake saw me and he knew I was still in a state of shock; and not there at least not yet. He felt at one time what I was feeling and knew it. Smiling to me he diverted people away from me until I felt more conscious and re-connected to get involved with what obviously was going on.

What I needed was separation, so after walking over to my Harley then getting my helmet on; I fired her up, and headed out for a drive hoping that would help. The breeze felt warm against my body I could feel it on my hands and the back of my neck as I throttled the bike faster.

Amazingly the ride did help me a little I mean my senses came back to where I could hear things better.

Stopping about 5 miles or so up from the house I found an old trail we used to walk just Lori-Ann and I to talk about things; it helped to clear both our heads walking hand and hand together; sadly, though this walk I started was alone, but I smiled feeling her spirit beside me.

Listening I heard the birds in the trees chirping away. Looking to my right I spotted a couple of chipmunks running around a log. The breeze as on my motorcycle still felt warm and light as it kissed my face.

Smiling once more I walked back to my Harley, got my Helmet back on. Re-firing my Motorcycle back up throttling it faster heading for home again. Pulling back into the driveway Snake watched me from the balcony jumping off my bike with a better spring in my step he smiled as I caught it smiling back he knew I was back to Rock.

Meanwhile back once again beneath Vermont's famed Sable Mountain. A very tired and worn out Lori-Ann was being carried out of that room she had been currently held in, and back down the corridor.

The combination of sweat and urine could be smelt throughout, as she could be seen being carried into the shower room to bath.

Where immediately after having her feet placed down upon the tiled floor. Her eyes were re-introduced once again to the strange green hypnotic lights, as before making her mind not her own Being handed a bar of soap a different attendant could be heard next saying.

"Go; take a shower; and clean everywhere slave; Do you understand?"

Just before walking away himself to wait for her; the attendant grins and watches as Lori-Ann turning on her toes slowly then proceeding into the steaming droplets but not before replying.

"Yes Master, I hear, and will obey."

As the steaming water kissed her bare skin it lightly danced upon her body. Lori continued using the soap lathering up everywhere, as she had been commanded to do. Being seen re-emerging herself several times; until her body squeaked clean. However, without the simplest luxury of a towel to dry herself off with; Lori merely stepped back out still dripping wet.

Shortly after re-placing her collar around her neck then re-attaching the leash Lori then lowered herself on her hands and knees, as the attendant lead her as most men there did with their slaves. As the other females crawled where ever they were being lead also.

The attendant knew he had to feed her now before she was to taken back away for phase 2 of Lori-Ann's torture.

Being seen standing in line may have made it look like an any cafeteria; that you'd see, but this particular one believe me was all to different. Here are just few examples to let you see why it's so.

First off, all the females in the line with their male counterparts knelt naked beside them. The males however wore ankle high boots and black leather shorts second…While the males waited for the food to feed their slaves. Their slaves however were assisted into adult sized highchairs where once inside of them their wrists were placed behind them where they were next handcuffed behind them. Their legs after were lifted out in front of them then placed on top of 2 6X6 construction columns where their ankles were then clamped. The third and last element of this cafeteria that makes it different are the naked rovers that lick the feet and suck upon the toes of one's being feed. These females are like the others completely naked but these women have all been specially programed to be foot worshiping pacifiers. Walking back over to her the attendant in-between moans of Lori-Ann began to feed her, as she smiled looking at him. The rover who had been given Lori-Ann's feet to lick and toes to suck upon happens to have been Brenda Davis as she knelt naked in front of Lori. I on the other hand found myself back at the house; regaining my precious balance once more after Lori's abduction that clearly rocked me mentally. But as I always say failure for me wasn't going to be an option now that I'm re-focused.

Having finally gotten myself back upstairs to say the least seeing my Uncle and cousin picking up my place for me left me feeling kind of guilty. Upon seeing me pitching in B.J. next decided to check out my upstairs for me just to make sure nothing up there was disturbed. But just like at F.B.I. headquarters my sixth sense decided to kick itself back into play once again shortly after picking up a towel supposedly worn by Lori-Ann. Naturally hearing the thud of me falling to my knees caused B.J. to come running halfway down the stairs. Standing there however he next watches me gripping the towel tighter which after closing my eyes the images began playing themselves out fully.

The very first image was of two men dressed in black entering the house through the kitchen. The second image I watched showed one of them chasing Lori-Ann around the living room having things being thrown at him, as Lori tried her best to evade being captured.

But witnessing the third image it showed Lori-Ann down on her knees just staring at the two green beams from some type of hypnotic device by the second man. The fourth and final image showed Lori-Ann with a leather collar around her neck attached to it was clipped a leash, shortly after dropping the towel Lori could be seen walking out being lead out by both men. Once again as before with the images stopping I collapsed exhausted on the floor.

As I continued laying there watching the images of Lori playing themselves out for me over and over again. It suddenly became apparent to me somehow my subconscious was trying to re-assure me that Lori-Ann was indeed alive. Though it did take me some time before I did wake up; it certainly didn't surprise me seeing the looks of concern upon everyone's face.

"Jesus Eddie, I certainly don't know how you do that; but it scared me when you fell are you all right?" Asked Uncle Jesse as I could be seen sitting up more upon the couch.

"Thanks Uncle Jesse, yes I'm all right thank god, sorry I scared you like that, but man what a set of visions that was?" I exclaimed sitting there.

"That's alright Eddie, were just glad you're OK. But do you think you can tell us about what you saw?" "Sure, well Lori was definitely taken by two guys dressed in black, they came in through the kitchen." "Could you tell anything more about them?"

"Sorry B.J. All the visions showed me was they were both dressed in black, and they were tall other than that there really wasn't much to see."

"Were they ninja's?"

"No Snake, they weren't ninja's, or they certainly didn't leave me with the impression they were." "Eddie did they say anything or do anything unusual that you saw?"

"Well, I did see one of them chasing Lori-Ann around here, luckily he couldn't catch her at first, then how could anyone catch my wife when she is throwing things at him. Then this second guy appeared suddenly next holding something in his hand.

Which stopped Lori in her tracks, but then that image flashed quickly to the next scene, so I couldn't make out what this second guy was holding exactly."

"You're doing great Eddie, I'm proud of you just take your time and try to tell us what happened in this next scene."

"Thanks Uncle Jesse, Well the next thing I saw was Lori-Ann with her towel completely off her body kneeling in front of this second man just starring at what looked like two green beams of light coming from something in this guy's hand but I really couldn't see it clearly sorry Uncle Jesse."

"What do have to be sorry for Eddie you did great, what you just said confirms that whatever device was used on Lori-Ann was also used on Stacy McKenna at F.B.I. headquarters earlier, but is that all you saw?"

Snake in the meantime extended his hand down to assist me up and off the couch.

It now wouldn't be until checking my watch to see it was 2:00P.M. before my telephone rang next; seeing it was Danny I took it immediately.

"Hello Danny what's up?"

"Hi Eddie, hope I'm not disturbing you, but I have a couple of things for you down here, think you can stop by the restaurant?"

"Yeah Danny sure we can, ah is it busy now?"

"No, it's not busy now."

"Great, were on our way." It wouldn't be until hanging up with Danny that Uncle Jesse exclaimed to us.

"Say Eddie, I've got to get back to headquarters, call me if you come up with anything else in this investigation?"

"You'll be the first to know Uncle Jesse thanks." Having said good-bye, we all watched Uncle Jesse leave.

"Well guy's feel like going to see Danny he said he had a couple of things down at the restaurant," Mutually seeing us all agreeing then leaving together.

Mid-day traffic seamed lighter than usual as we could be seen pulling into our perspective parking spaces behind the restaurant.

Spotting Danny coming out of the kitchen area we joined him at the counter.

"All right Danny, were here what's up pal?"

"Well, a couple of things actually, you know that license plate number you showed me earlier?" "Yeah, I remember?"

"Well I showed it around like I said I would, and you see that guy over there with the Hawaiian shirt on, he claims he can tell you all about it for a price sorry Eddie." Danny exclaimed as B.J. looked over at this individual in question.

"Excuse me Eddie, you mind if I take this guy for you, he's a local snitch I know?" Nodding my head, we watched B.J. walking over to the Hawaiian shirt guy; watching B.J. shaking this guy's hand he then sat beside this guy to hear what he had regarding the license plate number.

Turning our attention back to Danny, as Snake and I listened he exclaimed next.

"Listen Eddie, you see that table in the back without the light?"

"You mean the one I told you about the last time I was here; you still didn't get anyone to change that bulb?" Grinning I winked at Snake.

Reaching under the bar Danny hands me a bulb which I accept from him.

"Thanks for volunteering pal, ah why you over there you might want to talk with the guy there to, he says he needs help in locating his fiancé seams she's missing."

"Great, like I'm not already busy working on a case." I exclaimed walking past Danny and Snake. Usually if approaching anyone yet unseen, or unknown my sixth sense would alert me to danger if there was any. But as strange as it may sound, as I drew closer to this individual something felt amazingly recognizable about him.

Stopping I watched him getting up; his height was identical to my own; and even his build we appeared identical. But it wouldn't be until changing the bulb before the light showed just who it was sitting there. My twin brother Elvis Aaron and I mutual grabbed each other in a long-awaited hug.

"Look at you Elvis, all grown up, God if mom and dad could see us now reuniting after 20yrs I've really missed you." I exclaimed stepping back to get a better look at him.

"Thanks Eddie, can't say I haven't missed you either big brother it certainly has been a while." Watching him with his head down looking at the floor.

"Oh, by the way I think I owe your friend Danny some plates; he dropped them when I tried to explain to him I wasn't you." A quick smile came to my face as I exclaimed.

"Forget it Elvis I got you covered anyway he would've dropped them worse if you and I walked in here together remember?" Quickly Elvis could next be seen with a smile upon his face as he exclaimed back.

"Oh yeah I do, Mrs. Cutter right third grade, you know even though she had a hard time telling us apart it was still pretty fun confusing her like we did." We next could be seen laughing together after which things became serious when I next exclaimed.

"Danny tells me your fiancé is missing; I'm sorry to hear that Elvis would you like to talk about it maybe I can help? Who is she? Do I know her?" Watching him leaning back in his chair with his arms folded. I continued to observe him weighing out the option of telling him or not until he exclaimed.

"To tell the truth Eddie, I don't think you do, I first met her back in 1987 with her Father down in Miami.

Her dad was down there on a business trip, I was 26yrs old then but let me tell you when I saw her wearing that skimpy bikini big brother she instantly captured my heart."

Smiling to myself as I continued sitting there I knew exactly what my little brother was saying. "What were you doing in Miami when you first saw her?"

"Working actually for a hotel down there as a waiter/towel handler to tell you the truth Eddie I almost fell in the pool a few times whenever I'd walk past her laying there just sunning herself."

"That beautiful huh?"

"Beautiful, big brother she is drop dead gorgeous, she has these blue eyes, and long brown hair, and tall? She had to be six feet tall Eddie."

The more I listened to him describing her, the more it sounded like the young lady I was hired to locate. The bad news was my brother really didn't know what happened to her …Yet.

"Ah Elvis, tell me something your fiancés name wouldn't happen to be Brenda Davis, would it?" "What the, how did you know who she was Eddie?"

"Your description of her little brother, oh man now more than ever I really wish to hell I was wrong." "Wrong? What do you mean Eddie; your scaring me; has something happened to her I should know about?"

"I'm sorry about scaring you little brother, but yeah there has, but before I begin to tell you; I just want to know how prepared are you?" Seeing a much more puzzled and horrified look upon his face; I certainly hated like hell to be the one who told him, but hey I was his brother. Every so often Elvis would pull his seat out a little bit then moves it back into the table, as he continued listening to me.

Having recently gone through it myself. I thought it best to wait until I fully explained everything that had happened to his fiancé Before informing him of my own tragedy. Being joined by Snake and B.J they confirmed what I said.

CHAPTER FOUR

"Like I said before Elvis, I really wish to hell I was wrong, but listen if it's any consolation to you we do share an additional thing in common?"

Huh, What's that?"

"Whoever this sick bastard is who has your finance; he also has my wife as well." Shifting his eyes toward the others seeing B.J. and Snake nodding their heads in silent confirmation.

Excusing myself I placed an order in quickly with Danny ordering an assorted platter figured gave us all something to pick through while we kept talking.

"So, Eddie, tell me something how do I get on board with you guys in this investigation after all I do have an additional score to settle with this bastard?"

Even though it had been several minutes before deciding I finally exclaimed to him.

"Be cool little brother you're in, but I call the shots, you do what I say when I say It all right?" Catching a smile from Elvis looking back over to me we then heard him exclaim.

"Great; not even into a half hour of this reunion after twenty years, and he already has his big brother shtick scripted." Playfully I could be seen lightly tapping him on the back of his head as the food was being brought over to us.

"Eat smart ass or you don't get the keys to the car Saturday night."

Smiling now toward each other it seemed pretty much official team James had its final member. "Oh Eddie, that guy over at that table, you know the Hawaiian shirt dude, he had some interesting things to say about this Maxwell Escabar guy."

After taking a bite of my chicken finger, I returned my attention back to my cousin exclaiming to him.

"Oh, really like what?"

"Well first off he told me he used to be a security guard at Bellevue Hospital in New York City. Then he said to me he remembers this one patient who always wore a hockey goaltenders mask said his name was Maxwell Escabar."

Being quick to make a connection I pulled out a copy of that license plate number handing it over to B.J. as I chewed my food.

"That's him, this guy also said to me; that part of Bellevue's rehab program the patients used to do arts and crafts, but this Escabar's thing was making license plates. He remembers seeing him making one exactly like that out of fabric."

It wouldn't be until swallowing my food in my mouth before I asked.

"In the statement, you made before you said was Maxwell Escabar, what did you mean by that?" Holding up his fingers while still chewing after B.J. Exclaimed.

"Well like I said before at Police Headquarters earlier he's dead Eddie don't you remember?" With the others shooting me a look I leaned back in my seat then said.

"Yes, now I remember you did mention that to me before B.J. Sorry dude; I completely forgot; so, did this guy say anything as to how Escabar died?

"Medical examiners report says he died in a suspicious fire in his room."

In his hospital room? That is suspicious? Were there any witnesses to see who may have started it?" "Just two maintenance men who ran into this guy when he was doing rounds about that time. He said they were in the vicinity of Escabar's room when they accidently ran into this guy coming back from a break together; but that's not all apparently this guy also told me that when the fire department did find Escabar He was laying on his bed on just the metal springs burnt beyond recognition."

Leaning back in my chair with my arms folded in front of me; starring just thinking to myself just how strange this was indeed. Noticing it was just about 4;00PM we all got up to leave the restaurant. I quickly discovered according to Sue Chang that my money wasn't any good. Smiling I kissed her for head thanking her for being so generous. Before being the last to leave I slipped Hawaiian shirt two hundred dollars in his shirt pocket for the information he provided us. Mentioning to me once we had gotten outside that he suddenly had a craving for a big apple Snake left saying he would catch us on the flipside back at my house later tonight.

B.J. Also mentioned to us that he needed to leave too. He explained to my brother and I that he needed to get back to F.B.I. Headquarters. Also saying that he'd catch up with us at the house later; leaving Elvis and I alone there.

"Listen Elvis, with everything that's happening, and all to both of us, and also given the fact that we will be working together. I'd like to invite you to stay with me at our home.

If of course you haven't already made arrangements for yourself that is yet.

Besides I hate to admit it; but if I were go home by myself I just might end up throwing things around or something over this abduction thing." Watching him smiling toward me with his head down.

"Thanks Eddie, I except your invitation, but like you I guess I'm afraid of being alone myself; I don't know really don't trust myself with my emotions the way they are after hearing about Brenda."

"Hey, were blood will get through this, you aren't going anywhere and neither am I" Giving him another hug we then got into each of our vehicles and headed to my house. Minutes passed before we could each be seen pulling our respective vehicles into my driveway might have been one thing. But for my poor neighbors seeing a second version of me getting out of a second vehicle might just need to explained somehow.

Laughing hysterically as we entered my home it wouldn't be until closing the door before Elvis exclaimed.

"Your poor neighbors, did you see their reaction as we…. Hello Nurse, is this? Having never actually had the pleasure of meeting Lori-Ann, Elvis paused from saying anything further to gaze upon the self portrait of Lori-Ann on the wall of the furrier to my house.

"Yes, little brother; that's her; that's your sister-in-law what do you think?"

"Think? Are you kidding me Eddie I'm floored she's as gorgeous as Brenda is big brother."

"Thanks Elvis, yeah I kind of asked Lori-Ann if she wouldn't have minded wearing the same outfit she wore on the day we first met at the Williamsburg Fair grounds."

I had to admit even though the portrait of her was unconventional the photo in question had Lori wearing her tight blue jean shorts, in addition she had on her Van Halen half shirt that showed off her very slender waist line, I so fondly remember her wearing on that joyous day poised in a sitting position on a white fence barefoot.

Standing their humbly I thought to myself this was defiantly was a GQ type scenario. But what the heck it was most reminiscent for me having first seen Lori-Ann back then in the summer of 1982 at the fairground.

Thinking back to what Elvis had said about us just reuniting about an hour ago wasn't fiction, but sadly fact. It has been years since we last seen each other.

But believe me as I watched him taken an interest in what I was telling him about his future sister-in-law in all honesty I felt that space in time starting to shrink.

Having completed the grand tour of the house some forty minutes later. We next could be seen walking together about a mile and a half away to the hidden quarry where Lori-Ann and I usually found ourselves skinny dipping in.

"Listen Eddie, I've got to say this, I'm really proud of you have a gorgeous home, and a very beautiful wife, but hey I just want to thank you also for letting me stay with you; honestly I really appreciate it." Feeling his arm slipping behind my back; I returned mine to his silently symbolizing our reunion to be completed.

But while my brother and I continued our ultimate bonding experience they're on the rock ledge. Our cousin unfortunately was finding himself in a situation back at F.B.I. Headquarters just after a surprise locker inspection by a fellow agent Jerome Givens.

"Givens!! I should have known it was you, just tell me what the meaning of this is?" Standing there with his knee in B.J.'s back was first year special agent Jerome Givens.

"What the meaning of this is? Well I found myself doing a very random locker inspection and while a majority of them were clean as a whistle, I can't say the same for yours, now can I? Holding in his hand was a small baggie of what looked to be cocaine. B.J. then caught the smuggest look from him as Givens looked at my cousin.

"Listen to me you little snot nosed, ass kissing, jealous prick, I've never seen that stuff before in my life, but hey let me give you a little reality check huh, if I find out this is your idea of a set-up be warned paybacks a bitch." Together each of them could be seen starring each other down.

"What the Sam Hell is going on here!" Boomed a loud voice walking toward them rounding the corner was none other than F.B.I. Director Tex McKenna.

"Gladly Sir, Well I was in the process of doing a random locker inspection and while a majority of them were clean I happened upon this agent's locker when I discovered this sir?" Turning his smug head toward B.J.

"Hmm, I see well agent James is this true?" McKenna then turned his attention back toward B.J. "No Sir it certainly is not true, begging the directors pardon but I'm being wrongly accused of something

I don't nor would ever consider doing in my life Sir." Exclaimed B.J. Struggling against agent Givens.

Minutes however passed while McKenna could be seen thinking of what to do next, obviously he couldn't blame Agent Givens for jumping the gun, after all it was a crime to be in the possession of an illegal substance.

"Take his gun and badge then read him his Miranda Rights." As McKenna turned and started walking out of the locker room B.J. exclaimed Loudly

"THIS IS BULLSHIT!!" But while B.J was going through the booking process miles away Snake was at that very moment taken a bite out of the big apple literally. (Taking the interstate straight going west Snake arrived to begin his search.)

Snake cruised the NY streets after getting a tip from a guy who owed him for helping him out of a tricky situation. The tip regarded two biological brothers by the name Oswald. According to Snake's snitch who was 99% right most of the time Johnny and Tommy were the very maintenance men who worked at Bellevue Hospital around the time of Maxwell Escabar's supposed death.

Ever so patiently Snake just waited and watched in the shadows of New York's underbelly of the city for the brothers to surface.

Tommy Oswald not only was the younger of the brothers but the shorter one of the two, only standing 5'7" but sadly he was a poker with a gut bigger than the Charles River at low tide. Johnny Oswald on the other hand may have been taller and lankier, but sadly he found himself to be stupider than his younger brother.

If Johnny wasn't trying to talk Tommy into a night of drinking, Johnny was talking Tommy into scoring a fix for themselves to shove into their arms. In any event these two were looking at being candidates for matching black body bags and in addition to the toe tags as well. Seeing them stopping just up ahead of him; Snake continued slithering up the side of the alley wall.

"WELL NOW!" Exclaimed Snake from behind them from within the shadows of the alley way. As they stumbled forward into the trash cans smashing their glass fix on the ground.

"Jesus Christ Snake, What the hell you doing?" Exclaimed Tommy toward Snake. "Well I would say I gave two shits about you two losers but I can't lie, so I don't."

"I am here however for intel which I know you'll provide me with or else?"

Having dealt with Snake's temper before it didn't take Johnny Oswald long to sing about everything he knew much to Tommy Oswald's best effort to shut his brother up.

"Way to go big brother I hope you realize were dead men when you know who finds out we betrayed him like this" Tommy exclaimed over toward his brother.

"Listen Tommy, for all we know Mr. you know who could be half way around the world for all we know. Besides I've seen Snake's temper before when others have refused to answer his questions, and let me tell you little brother I did the right thing in telling him" Johnny exclaimed back toward Tommy, as Johnny next watched Snake nodding his head toward Johnny.

"See Tommy Johnny here isn't as dumb as you look, well ladies thank you for the intel and I'll be catching you on the flipside." Snake said as he mysteriously vanished from their site.

Having gotten back to his car Snake immediately started back to Massachusetts once again with the information he had received by Johnny Oswald.

Meanwhile back in Boston at F.B.I. Headquarters we had all gathered to await the release of our cousin. Who in my personal opinion was being conveniently set-up for something but sadly as to what; still wasn't clear to me, at that moment.

Within a matter of minutes however we all watched him being escorted out to the front desk sergeant to sign for his things. Knowing enough not to say anything until we were all outside we watched B.J.

Holding it in, but believe me if you were received a stare from a James Boy the way we were seeing it at that moment. You'd certainly want to run for your life.

"Dad, I swear there is no way I'm just going to sit back while these bureaucratic idiots try to railroad me on some bullshit drug possession charge like this." B.J. Expressed in an aggravated tamed down voice just low enough for us to hear.

"Calm down Robert please son, we believe you, your right this is a bullshit charge that someone's conveniently labeled you with absolutely you should fight it."

"What do you suggest I do about it?"

"Well until we can prove otherwise, I suggest you lay low, and let me see if I can get to the bottom of this from my end. Help your cousin out on this case keep your skills sharp." Considering what his father said to him it certainly did make sense thinking about helping us.

Besides uncle Jesse was right it would give him a chance to try and figure things out from his end.

"Hey cuz, remember all those football games I came to watch you play in your senior year of high school.

Well back then you showed opposing offences no mercy in getting through those lines.

"Now your dad's right in suggesting you help us because the opposing team I'm facing is kicking my ass, so I could use your toughness to break through.

It wouldn't be until catching him with a fond reflective smile upon his face of those glory days before we could hear him say to us.

"Blood Takes Care of Blood…. No Matter What." After which we gave each other a group hug sealing our family pact.

It might have looked strange to see four men hugging but in reality, you had to be a James Boy.

It took us minutes of saying good-bye to each other before we each could be seen leaving F.B.I. Headquarters.

"Sure, is a bum rap what happened to B.J." Elvis exclaimed watching me drive.

"Sure, is little brother, but Uncle Jesse is right about this being a bullshit charge conveniently being placed upon B.J. And he was right in having him working with us." Watching Elvis nodding his head in agreement.

"Oh yeah hell I'd dig working with him, but tell me something between you and I who do you think set him up?"

Hearing Elvis asking that was defiantly a good sign that he was concentration on something other than his fiancé's abduction.

"Hard to say who did it little brother, to tell you the truth though anyone could've done it who held a grudge against him. But what I couldn't understand was why Tex McKenna was smiling while B.J. was collecting his things from the desk sergeant?"

Shooting me a quick look over Elvis could be heard replying back.

"Dam Eddie I thought I was the only one who spotted that?" Smiling back at him I replied back. "No sorry little brother, I caught that also myself, but what I can't figure out is why?"

It might have been a little past ten thirty in the evening when we could be seen pulling my car into the driveway right behind Snake's Lamborghini.

Though it wouldn't be until getting out before our nasal passages were overcome by the aroma of food coming from of all places the pool area.

Seen opening the gate my brother and I see Sue Chang there serving up food she had skillfully prepared at her restaurant.

But as Elvis could be seen passing me to check out the food there, I on the other hand still stood there in utter amazement. As I next felt a gentle tug on my pant leg.

"Listen Eddie, please don't be upset with Sue for wanting to do this for you. It's just well we heard about what happened to Lori-Ann, and wanted to do something for you, you know to help you out." Smiling I just watched the others eating thinking to myself this absolutely was the nicest gesture anyone had ever done for me given the situation my brother and I were in.

After helping myself to some chicken wings, some pork friend rice, and a couple of egg rolls; before I snuck up behind Sue then said. "Hey Sue, I just want to thank you for doing this; Elvis and I really appreciate it more than you know."

Leaning in I kiss her softly on the cheek. "Your very welcome Eddie, but listen you don't have to thank me for all your friendship you've given me over the years this is an honor for me." Seeing her leaning back to kiss me too, I slowly stepped back away from her as our lips separated.

Finding a seat beside Snake he began telling me of where he had gotten back from.

"Just got back from a road trip of sorts?"

"Really Where to?"

"The big apple New York City, got a tip from one of my stoolies about the two brothers who used to be employed at Bellevue Hospital?"

"Ah huh, and?"

"Let's just say I got one of them to sing for me real pretty." "Really what did he say?"

"He informed me that the body the authorities found wasn't Escabar's for one thing." "Interesting."

"Yes, isn't it, according to this one brother Maxi was switched with another patient who died about the same time he escaped."

"Switched how, body wise?

"Affirmative, but not just in body, but also his medical records were presto changed as well, so?"

"So, the M.E. receives the body along with the medical records simply writing it off as Escabar without a thorough autopsy."

"Exactly."

"All right well did this singing brother happen to explain then how Escabar managed to escape?" "Naturally, in all the confusion with the fire department this guy along with his half-witted brother managed to smuggle Escabar out in a waiting laundry truck." "That makes sense."

"Absolutely"

"So, we know he was switched with someone else, and also the M.E. officially wrote it off as him, but then he successfully escapes from Bellevue, but now here comes the $64.00-dollar question who did he kill to get originally put in there to begin with?

Still watching however he looked to have been in the process of telling me when a more recognizable person could be heard clearing his throat behind us.

Turning around we spot Uncle Jesse standing there. Snake and I then watched as he next could be seen placing an ordinary folder down on my poolside table before making his way back to us.

"Pardon me Eddie for interrupting, but I believe that I may be able to answer that particular question better than Snake could, no offence to you of course."

Conceding to Uncle Jesse, Snake bows toward him out of complete respect for his authority. "All right Uncle Jesse, I'll pose the question to you then, why is it so difficult in finding any written confirmation on the first-degree murder conviction of Maxwell Escabar that sentenced him to life at Bellevue Hospital, and who did he kill?"

Snake stood just behind my Uncle, where together we noticed Elvis coming up to listen in hopes of hearing the answer as well. Not meaning to at first; I found myself starring up toward Uncle Jesse in hopes he would enlighten us with something resembling an answer.

"Oh Boy, I always knew this day would come when I'd have to answer these questions, but I was always hoping that anybody but my nephew would be the asking me about it.

"But listen boy's I've always meant to tell you, but never could bring myself around to doing it, and I'm truly sorry. For the things, you're about to finally find out about Maxwell Escabar." It wouldn't be until getting up then walking over toward the table that I next picked up the folder.

Glancing at its contents like I was doing; my eyes quickly shut instantly as my sixth sense kicked itself in once more there.

The first image showed me as a young boy having my hair tasseled by dad playfully after reminding me to be good and listen to my Uncle before watching him walking across the street over to his car.

The second image that flashed showed me running back to the front porch to stand next Elvis and Uncle Jesse as the three of us waved good-bye to then mouthing I love you to both of them; they mouthed back they each loved us to.

The third and final image however caused me to cringe; as we watched the car tragically exploding across the street from the house.

Though Uncle Jesse naturally tried his best to turn us away from seeing it burning any further sadly and equally tragic the damage had already been done.

I knew there just had to be more to explain of why Uncle Jesse kept this painful truth from me all these years since it happened. But as I finally opened my eyes to not seeing my brother standing beside me any more I feared the worst.

Fanning out the others searched for him; knowing him however from when we were younger obviously I had a pretty good idea he hadn't of gotten far.

It wouldn't be until I ventured to my cellar before I came upon him in my dojo.

Seeing him sitting on one of my practice mats; I sat myself crossing my legs in a lotus position across from him as he exclaimed to me.

"I really don't understand human nature at all big brother; why did he have to tell us who killed mom and dad for?" Watching my heavy bag swinging kind of left with the impression he hauled off on it in a heated flurry shortly after seeing our parents name there in that file.

"Human nature huh, that's a very complicated subject Elvis to tell you the truth I sometimes have problems with that myself; but let me see if I can answer your question for you huh, my guess of why he did that was more because of me?" Shaking his head after giving me a look he next exclaimed.

"Come on Eddie I'm not going blame you for this."

"Why not I'm the supposed investigator digging up these facts concerning the disappearance of this young lady your fiancé. Establishing not only proof of what happened, and how it happened, but just who may have done this. So, in essence I kind of blame myself for Uncle Jesse showing us that file outside."

"Yes, but Eddie even though we may have seen that this Maxwell Escabar did according to that file of Uncle Jesse's. Did kill mom and dad in that car explosion; come on I'm never going to blame you for doing your job."

"Thanks, little brother I appreciate that, but believe me if I've been going through this in my own way since it happened. I can only imagine what it's done to you over the years."

"No Eddie don't say that you used to say that when we were kids remember, but believe me you're a lot stronger. Than I am dealing with this as a martial artist but you can't imagine how I've felt."

"Gee Elvis your absolutely right, I apologize for thinking or even saying that I did understand, because believe it or not you and I have been blessed with another opportunity at being brothers, and I'm not ready nor will I ever throw in the towel on us."

Seeing him reaching his hand out for mine, I reciprocated extending mine out to him, as well as I watched him crying there.

Gazing up the stairs I could see the others smiling as they looked down upon us, consoling one another like we were; I then sent back up to them a gentle smile of my own. Silently indicating that things would eventually work themselves out.

Miles away however Lori-Ann found herself having been granted the littlest of mercies from her captor. For not being able to supply him with any information on the case I was working on.

Still unfortunately found herself a prisoner in his demented realm of sleaze; fearfully awaiting her pending fate to be re-established once more.

"Oh God, now where in the hell am I this time?" Exclaiming to herself as she could be seen slowly sitting up on the soft cot she had been lying upon.

"All right Lori-Ann think…. assess the situation your still in now…. your still naked obviously…. you're in an 8X10 room laying on a soft military cot…. with an extremely long vertical mirror in front of you….

With what looks like three camera's hanging above the mirror." Pausing Lori hears the softest moans coming from inside the room with her.

"Oh my God!" There laying directly beneath the mirror was none other than Brenda Davis.

Light headed when she first got herself up and off the cot Lori could be seen momentarily closing her eyes until the dizziness went away.

Next Lori could be seen walking over to kneel beside Brenda. Turning her gently Lori next could be seen resting Brenda's head upon her knees as she begins to awaken.

"NO get away, get away from me don't tickle me again, I beg you don't!" Lifting herself up somehow Brenda next could be seen crawling away to an opposite corner to cower before Lori who just continued sitting there perplexed.

"No hey wait I'm not going to tickle you honey believe me I'm as much a victim in this hell as you are." Still terrified the young lady merely nods her head in Lori's direction. "Really? You're sure you're not going to?"

Watching Lori with a friendly smile shaking her head no to her. Caused Brenda naturally first to breathe a sigh of relief as she could be seen giving Lori a half smile back. "Listen whoever you are; I first can't tell you what that means to hear you're not a well you know; and I'd like to apologize to you also for my reaction before." As both ladies continued smiling toward one another.

Each suddenly felt a little more comfortable for the first time since their capture.

"To tell you the truth honey, you really don't have to apologize to me for your reaction before I completely understand this place frightens you." Once more their warmest smiles continued to comfort the other lady as they sat there.

"You want to hear something funny?" Exclaimed Lori-Ann with her legs crossed in front of her. "Sure, what's that not that I could use a laugh about now." Replied Brenda back to Lori. "Ah first you might want to retract that last statement if I were you." Lori watches as Brenda realizes just what she had said.

"Hey Psycho tickler wherever you are? I was kidding before if you're listening ah that was a figure of speech not to be taken seriously." Carefully the two watch for any kind of repercussions, but after discovering there wasn't any they next could be seen giggling amongst themselves.

"God that felt so good saying that thank you for suggesting that, but now what was that thing you were going to say before that you'd thought I'd find funny?"

"Oh that, well I was just thinking ever since we've been in this room together neither of us has introduced themselves yet?" Exclaimed Lori-Ann getting up off of the floor.

"You know something you're absolutely right; we've been so busy worrying about this maniac, we never did get a chance to introduce ourselves to each other yet my names Brenda." Exclaimed Brenda getting herself up off of the floor.

"It's a pleasure to meet you Brenda my names Lori-Ann,"

But as the two of them could be seen mutually hugging the other suddenly from out of nowhere the two ladies could hear the clapping of hands, as Brenda next could be seen with a horrified expression upon her face gazing back over toward Lori-Ann.

"Oh no Lori not again it's him I'm afraid." Burying her body close into Lori-Ann. Lori feels Brenda trembling with freight.

"Brenda, listen to me we are going to get out of here trust me; this is his sick game he's playing with us. But once my husband finds this place he will free us from this manic."

CHAPTER FIVE

"**B**ut trust me we can't give up hope that we will not be freed, because if we do give up. that hope of ever being freed; listen to me Brenda, then he wins." As Lori finishes her pep talk to the young lady.

Brenda next could be seen lifting her head to a smiling Lori looking sweetly down upon her.

"Bravo, Bravo Mrs. James that indeed was an eloquent speech.

My compliments to you on being an effective speaker.

However, I do have to correct you on just a couple of flaws you did make.

Your first delusional my dear if you think you're going to be freed, because sad to say it, but that will never happen.

Your second delusional flaw is this misconception you have of your husband actually finding you, because trust me he won't."

"Save your bullshit there for someone who gives a fuck because we don't.

Oh, and if anyone is delusional here it is you. Your sick fuck it isn't us, because we will be freed that you can count on.

And another thing on the subject of my husband; you underestimate him, and his ability greatly in locating this hell hole.

Because he will find this place; and when he doses; Let's just say I certainly wouldn't want to be you." Impressed once again by my wife's continued defiance over him all their captor could really do was smile as he continued watching them.

It certainly wouldn't be until after fully contemplating his next move. Before their mysterious captor could be seen pushing what looked to be an ordinary button on his console directly in front of him.

There inside this room in actuality what he has done was re-place Brenda as well as Lori-Ann back under his mindless control once more.

"I've come to a conclusion ladies on just what to do with you, but before I go into divulging that, I'd like to command the two of you to get down on your knees now. as you keep your eyes focused on my beams of light still shinning into them Do You understand?"

Observing his two slaves slowly dropping to their knees before him. He continues listening, as they reply back to him in unison. "Yes Master, we hear, and we obey." Grinning once more to himself their captor continues watching the green hypnotic beams.

"That's right ladies you have no fears and absolutely no defiance towards me is that understood ladies?" Watching them nodding their heads yes, he hears them repeating back just what they previously said before.

With Brenda, still on her knees there with no fear in her; Lori-Ann also could be seen on her knees beside her completely submissive now toward her Master. As he now sat there with his arms folded just watching his attendants as they could be seen now placing mind altering helmets upon each of the ladies' heads. He now could be seen sitting there behind his console flicking a yellow switch to activate them. But now as their mysterious captor puts his feet up to watch his slaves continuing to be brainwashed there before him.

Back, at the house however we all could be seen adjourning back down into my office to finally listen as Uncle Jesse begins to explain just why our parent's killer was never revealed to us before tonight.

"Before I begin to tell you about your parent's killer; I just want to re-state just how sorry I am for not telling either of you this painful truth sooner before tonight. But you have to believe me boys being thrown into being responsible as your guardian shortly after that tragedy pretty much scared me to death, and that you have to believe me".

"But back then all I was concerned with was protecting you boy's from making the same mistake as Maxwell Escabar had in his demented revenge against me which sadly he was successful in achieving," Watching him hanging his head in shame caused B.J. To kneel before him to ask.

"Dad, how come you never told me about it?" Looking into his father's eyes he watched as he shook his head toward him.

"I don't know son; I really don't know?" Watching his father like he was B.J. then figured an explanation was about to take place. Could be seen stepping away to sit back down to my left, along with Elvis seated to my right.

I suddenly felt for a moment; like a second judge at a court martial hearing. As we watched Uncle Jesse next moving his chair directly in front of us. So that he could face the three of us a lot more easily.

"There that's much better; sitting in front of you boy's like this makes it a lot easier for me to answer questions I know you'll be asking me. So, let me start at the beginning; I can still remember it like it was yesterday; Several years prior to arresting Maxwell Escabar on a mister meaner when I shot and killed his Father in an act of self-defense".

"I'll never forget it was another cold Saturday night; the date was November 12th 1960 my partner and I received a call from dispatch to respond to a 3-11 in progress at the bank.

I remember we pulled up; just as they were running out, so my partner and I gave chase on foot pursuit for three blocks until they decided to duck into an alley.

I next remember breaking away from my partner taking the left side; while he worked his way up the right side.

I'd taken a bullet in my left shoulder knocking me down, as I next watched the two suspects thinking they had taken me out going after my partner.

I saw myself somehow ignoring the pain in my shoulder to make it back to my feet hunched over like I was I managed to sneak up on them about the same time, as they were about to take out my partner.

All I could remember was getting off two shots into them before I saw myself collapsing next there in front of my partner."

"So what happened dad; did you kill them?" Asked B.J. Looking at his Father.

"Yeah, believe it or not son my sergeant came by and told me they dug two bullets out of each of their chests." While my brother and I looked at each other impressed with Uncle Jesse's marksmanship.

It naturally didn't surprise our cousin seeing that his dad used to train as a long-distance sniper in the Marine Corp. Uncle Jesse mentioned to me once; about this one time years ago when he nailed this apple out of a tree from two thousand yards away.

"So what happened; this kid sought revenge for his father's death after ten years, and conveniently picked you huh?" Exclaimed Elvis toward Uncle Jesse.

"Well Elvis it certainly wasn't out of convenience that he picked me but all I could imagine was he must have overheard me describing to his mother what had happened that brought about his father's death."

"How old was this Escabar kid, at the time Uncle Jesse nine years old?" "Yes, Eddie exactly that's right he was nine."

"So, let's see if I have this straight; you're telling me this kid held some kind of grudge for ten more years against you huh?"

"As sad as it is to hear Elvis yes, it seemed that way after I confronted him in the alley near by the Fenway six months after your parent's funeral."

Elvis, B.J. and I watched, as Uncle Jesse first closed his eyes then began telling us about that most revealing night.

"I remember being on patrol shortly after my return to the department near the Fenway who knew it would have been him; but it was.

Knowing my state of mind back then; at the time, I thankfully called for immediate backup to assist me Sargent McKendric responded.

Together we began walking down the alley listening to him talking to himself in a loud voice bragging to himself about the incident six months ago."

Pausing to fix us some coffee we continued listening; as I could be seen passing out the hot cups. "Believe me boy's; it took all my restraint as a police officer not just kill him there myself."

"I Bet it did Uncle Jesse; but you want to hear something; if it were me I certainly wouldn't have had a problem doing it." Clearly with a serious look upon his face. Uncle Jesse just shakes his head to him; at the same time replying back.

"Elvis, Maxwell Escabar carefully waited for ten long years before executing his revenge against me for killing his father".

"Because revenge no matter what the circumstances is never an excuse to see anyone die for; because in its tragic wake it only leaves behind casualties."

"Two wrongs never make any bad situation right."

"That's correct Eddie; yes exactly."

"So, Uncle Jesse tell us about what happened next?"

"Well as Sargent McKendric and I drew ourselves upon him we continued listening to Escabar bragging about just how successfully he planted that bomb in your parent's car."

"We then overheard him laughing to himself. As he went on to verbally describe the horrified looks upon the faces of the people around there when they heard the explosion."

"Needless to say shortly after placing him under arrest for being extremely drunk. The detectives stepped up their efforts to obtain a search warrant then only after an extensive search were those mister meaner charges replaced with two counts of felony murder in the first degree."

Watching Elvis getting up from his seat there; we next observed him walking back towards my dojo again in the deepest of thoughts. Shortly after discovering the truth about our parent's killer.

"Think Elvis will be all right?" Asked Uncle Jesse with a concerned look upon his face.

"Think Elvis just needs time Uncle Jesse like I do." Seconds before leaving him I find myself just listening to Uncle Jesse saying.

"Listen Eddie; for what it's worth you have to believe me if I could have told you about this before. I would've I only thought in both your best interests I only did this to protect you both."

Feeling his eyes watching me walking pass him; I proceeded next to join my brother inside of my home studio. Uncle Jesse however could only watch us sitting together.

But while my brother and I continued doing our best to deal with this latest news flash concerning our parent's deaths.

None of us were aware of the meeting that was, at that moment taken place deep beneath Vermont's famed Sable Mountain.

"Good morning Mr. McKenna, first off I'd to thank you for not only meeting me at this most unusual hour, but also in taken care of that rodent problem within the bureau you were having."

"Yeah whatever; you have the money?"

"Of course, per our agreement fifty thousand dollars here it is."

"Thanks." McKenna next could be seen placing the oversized envelope into his inside jacket pocket. After which McKenna then produces another candidates list of potential victims for Escabar's demented realm of sleaze.

"Excellent, thank you again Mr. McKenna for your continued support not to mention keeping up your end of our agreement; now however I'm just wondering if you had any interests in seeing my latest accomplishments?" Curious enough in just wanting to get out of there; Tex McKenna continues to wait to view his hosts latest triumph.

Suddenly his facial expression changed dramatically upon viewing the four ladies in the before mentioned room.

"As you can see Mr. McKenna I have been quite busy with the other list you gave me last time, but if you'll allow me the pleasure of introducing you to my latest acquisitions."

There before him Tex watches as his very own nieces Gina Prescott, and Trish Davenport having not only their toes sucked but the souls of their feet could be seen also being sensually licked by none other than Brenda and Lori-Ann.

"You sick perverted bastard look what your subjecting my two nieces too; how could you?"

"Come on Mr. McKenna you of all people should know that my business includes the re-training and selling of my slaves." But while Tex McKenna continued watching the horror within that very room along with his perverted host.

Elvis and I however continued our best efforts to try and get some sleep much to our disappointment. Though despite our best efforts to get comfortable we had managed to get only four hours of sleep the time now was 4:30A.M. When we could be seen heading down stairs together.

"Looks like we still think the same huh?"

"Looks like it big brother; ah you want to get the coffee going?"

"Sure thing." Together Elvis and I set about to begin our first full day by preparing a power breakfast. "Hey, why are we sharing the cooking duties for, you're the guest: I should be cooking for you."

"Save it big brother I'm on a roll: could you pass me the milk please?" Reaching in I retrieved the milk handing it to him.

"Thanks; now get the bacon huh the pans hot enough." Standing there sure I may have just wanted to shoot the shit with him; but of course, that wouldn't have helped in addressing the problem he still had since that meeting last night with Uncle Jesse.

"Say Elvis; ah I was wondering if you might answer a question for me?" Carefully as I poured myself a coffee; I next could be seen pouring Elvis one as well.

Best thing I really still dug about my brother was that we were indeed so identical heck he took his coffee exactly like me with just milk, and two sugars.

Naturally it wouldn't be until we had a chance to sit down before I next could be seen smiling at him handing him his coffee cup.

"Sure, Eddie you can ask me a question if you'd still like to I don't mind."

"Great, thanks ah let's see I guess my only question is about that reply you made last night to Uncle Jesse; do you remember it?"

"Sure, I remember it, oh I get it, and you're probably wondering if I was serious about killing this guy, right?"

"Well you know that thought has been on my mind most of the night little brother."

But it wouldn't be until giving me the subtlest of smiles getting up once again to re-check our breakfast that he still was cooking before I heard saying back.

"Listen Eddie, I'd like to be able to tell you, yeah sure; absolutely; I was only kidding before with you and Uncle Jesse last night; when I said that I would've killed Escabar for the deaths of mom and dad. But back then I was too young to do anything about it. However now twenty years later; I'm sorry to be the one to tell you this big brother but my kid gloves are off now; and I am going to kill that cock roach."

Listening to hear my brother re-state exactly what he said to Uncle Jesse and I earlier naturally should have sent chills up my spine, but sadly it hadn't. Probably because deep down within me somewhere I too wanted him dead also.

Officially this was deemed our first breakfast together since re-uniting yesterday afternoon, but as we began eating across from one another; I still couldn't get the fact that my brother was still considering death for Maxwell Escabar as his only option.

"Ah Elvis; not to put a damper on your supposed plan to kill Escabar like your claiming you want to; but I hate to be the one to point this fact out. But you do realize the laws certainly not look upon this as a mercy killing by any stretch of the imagination unless naturally it's in a self-defense situation."

Hating like hell to express the obvious like that to him; I certainly could see him reflecting upon his previous statement in his mind.

Nodding his head toward me with a half-smile upon his face. I kept a watchful eye upon him. Finishing ahead of me; Elvis next could be seen getting back up to grab another coffee before leaving to shower first.

But while I remained there cleaning up after us my mind couldn't help but think of Lori in the sadistic hands of this maniac Maxwell Escabar. However rather than getting angry or upset about it I simply tried to re-focus my thoughts on just what we needed to do to get both our ladies back.

The time was just a couple minutes after six in the morning before I could be seen coming out the back door to join Elvis in a pre-stretching ritual almost every martial artist puts themselves through before any type of a run. But just as we continued preparing for ours.

Across town however our cousin could be seen sitting in his truck with his binoculars positioned on the residence of his former boss Tex McKenna. A ranch style house with a large garage located just to its left; as McKenna, next could be seen in his living room talking with someone on the phone at the same time pouring himself a scotch into a tumbler glass with ice. As a black Lincoln continental rolls up quietly behind him.

Lifting his eyes slightly B.J. Notices the driver through his rear-view mirror approaching on the passenger's side.

As the glasses fall slowly to his chest he listens as the door opens next wouldn't be until re-opening his eyes before B.J. could see his dad sitting there beside him.

"Good morning son."

"Good morning dad."

"Thought you could use a coffee so I got you one extra extra right?" "Yeah thanks dad"

"You're welcome son, you want something to eat; I got a couple of donuts here?"

Watching B.J. grabbing a chocolate one; Uncle Jesse smiles toward him knowing exactly how his son was feeling being blackballed by the bureau like he was.

"Listen dad; I appreciate the coffee and the donuts; but please don't tell me next I should leave this to you; that is until you listen to this first."

"Have you had a chance to count the money yet I gave you earlier?" "I'm counting it now as a matter of fact." "Good I'm glade hope it's all there?"

"Yeah me to; but to tell you the truth I do owe you an apology for what I said to you earlier."

"Forget it Tex; I mean if someone had just given me fifty thousand dollars for my two nieces and then proceeded to show me what I showed you earlier trust me; I probably would've called that guy a pervert too." As he watched his son switching off the recorder Uncle Jesse then listens to him exclaiming next.

"It certainly doesn't take a rocket scientist to figure out that old Tex is involved with someone dad." "Sure, seems that way son; but it's really too bad whoever Tex was talking with had some kind of voice changer."

It definitely made sense nodding his head in agreement with his father. B.J. naturally had his suspicion that suggested to him that muffled voice was of Maxwell Escabar. But whoever Tex was talking with clearly had some kind of device to eliminate all background sounds from where ever this other individual was from.

"So, in essence all you have for me to checkout is this your given me huh?"

"Actually, dad that tape is the one I gave you to have the lab boy's checkout; but I did manage to record something else you may want to listen too."

"Sheriff's office how can I help you?"

"It's Tex McKenna get me Agent Givens please."

"Morning boss thought you'd be calling me sooner or later what's up?"

"Just got back from a meeting thought I'd check in on your situation where your located care to give me a report yet?"

Well I'm happy to report first the sheriffs has been dealt with."

"That's great news; whew; now we can all breathe a sigh of relief thank you Jerome." "You're welcome; so, tell me how did your meeting go?"

"It went good as expected our benefactor got his list; and I got myself paid as usual for it with incentives." "Gotta love them huh; so, do you suspect he'll contact you""

"Can't say for sure maybe; yes." Watching his son shutting off the recorder uncle Jesse next replies. "Well, we already know the answer to that one doesn't we son?"

"Sure, do dad; now all we have to do is have the lab boys identify that other caller Tex was talking to on that first cassette tape I gave you." Nodding his head toward him Uncle Jesse leaves his son to head back toward police headquarters.

CHAPTER SIX

So, while Uncle Jesse, and B.J. Each made their way back to police headquarters to wait the results from the lab together.

Elvis and I were at that moment sprinting our way up the back-porch steps of the house. "Oh, wow Eddie, thank, thanks for inviting me to go with you that sure was great."

"Your welcome Elvis." Smiling toward each other I momentarily left him only to return within minutes carrying two large bath towels one I immediately handed him

After which I next placed down upon the table there; two bottles of water from the fridge. Smelling the morning air like I was, at that particular time always brought a smile to my face. As I

watched Elvis re-entering the house; I in turn just sat there in the deepest of reflections.

I had successfully defended my black belt in karate for the fifth and final time when I could be seen driving my Harley Davidson Motorcycle to attend Williamsburg's annual fair.

You're probably wondering why huh; I would come to something like this especially considering I wasn't married yet or had kids.

So, the answer to that's simple enough it kind of helps me remember and reconnect with my innocence growing up.

That's of course until tragedy reared its ugly head to snatch that precious innocence away from my brother and I.

Up until 1977 Uncle Jesse and I used to come to this every year; then of course circumstances made it impossible for either of us to attend.

I couldn't because of my competition schedule; Uncle Jesse couldn't because he'd often be on a stake-out; or he'd be assigned to protect a witness for the D.A. After four years of competitive competition from my previous life as a five-time martial arts champion I was ready to enjoy myself.

As I pulled into the parking lot; I wore my Van Halen tee shirt, blue jeans, chaps, and leather biker boots with the silver tips. I parked my Harley after circling a couple of times. As I stepped off I overheard a couple arguing

"You know something bitch; you really love embarrassing me in front of my boys here like this."

I tipped my mirrored sunglasses down to the edge of my nose. The young lady sat on a fence. With long brown hair, and killer blue eyes, she wore tight blue jean shorts, and the very same Van Halen tee shirt. I guessed her measurements were 36-24-36.

The guy who insulted her looked like an abusive, obnoxious twit. With long black hair, and a scraggly beard, and brown teeth. He sorts of resembled someone you'd see as maybe a national spokesman for psychos are us magazine.

"Carlos, let's see gee; I clean for you, cook for you, and even do your laundry for you, so I guess that entitles me to come here for a little fun; so, deal with it!"

I couldn't help but admire her for the way she stood up for herself. Honestly if I had a girlfriend I wouldn't want her to leave.

Turning around I removed my leather chaps. Suddenly he pushes her off the fence. Pushing her like that threw minding my own business out at that precise moment. I hurried up to the young lady.

"Are you, all right?" I took her hand pulling her up. Covered in thick mud my eyes couldn't escape the fact that this young lady was really still quite beautiful.

"Thank you…Yes I'm fine."

"Are you sure you're not hurt anywhere Miss?"

"Yes, I'm sure I think so at least; oh, sorry my names Lori-Ann and thank you for asking; but no, I'm pretty sure I'm not hurt anywhere at least not physically."

"Oh excuse me, Lori-Ann my name's Eddie by the way." "So much for me trying to enjoy myself here today."

I looked over at her boyfriend with his buddies still around him laughing. "Listen Lori-Ann; hold that thought before giving up on enjoying yourself here." As Lori was about to answer Carlos walked back over with his arms folded.

"Stranger if I were you I'd forget about helping her unless you really want to get hurt yourself for butting into something that's clearly none of your business." He poked me in the chest with his finger.

Uncle Jesse always used to tell me that people were always entitled to their own opinions; however, when a finger gets poked hard into your chest by a possessive twit like I was. Even Uncle Jesse would admit it was time to teach these guy's some manners Carlos hit me in the gut knocking me down on my knees.

"Alright Mr. For not taking the hint and minding your own business; my boys and I are going to teach you a painful lesson; so, you might want to take notes."

As another one picked me up and held me from behind one of his buddies continued hitting me in the stomach repeatedly. "Ah what's the matter hero that hurt?" Even though it might have believe me I was never going to acknowledge it to them.

"STOP IT CARLOS!! STOP IT!! YOUR GOING TO KILL HIM!!" ...." Shut up bitch you know something this is your fault." Laughing he watched me fall; but just before I hit the ground I suddenly flipped myself back up in a standing position.

"Alright now that you had a chance to beat on me a while unsuccessfully I might add...Let's see how your bozo's can take it; Come on Let's Dance."

I hit the first one to my left quick breaking his nose; and another hit after that with a stiff arm knocking him down to the ground.

"One down...three to go. Who's next?" The second one decided to charge me hopping to knock me off my feet but after flipping him up and over he fell hard crashing into the fence behind me.

"Ah Oh there goes number two down for the count." Smiling now we then saw the third friend making a well-timed exit running for his life out of the fairgrounds parking lot.

"Now that one was at least smarter; so, I guess it's just you and I Carlos hope you brought your dancing shoes?" But rather than engaging me himself, he too decided to make a run for it.

"Thank God" I dropped to one knee holding my left side.

"Eddie; oh my God." She ran up to me carefully placing her arm around me to try and help me up. "Your hurt I'm so so sorry are you…?"

"Please Lori thank you I'll be alright as long as no one punches me that is."

She gently wrapped her arm around me to help me up and I caught her warm smile casting itself over to me.

"Tell you what if you can give me a hand over to my bike then give me a couple of minutes I'll let you follow me to my nearby cabin; so, you can clean up. Then if you want to come back. I'll be more than happy to escort you around?"

Catching her playfully nod yes back to me; Lori assists me back over to my Harley.

"There you go; are you sure you can ride?" Slowly nodding my head, I next could be seen straddling it. "Why don't you go back to your car and just wait for me."

Allowing me the few minutes required I somehow could be seen firing it up driving out I waited for her.

Minutes passed before I did see her coming out, her car was a classic dark green Dodge Charger with a black stripe under both doors.

The good news was we really didn't have far to go from there; the bad new however was the only place Lori could really go to clean up was at the nearby quarry.

I was sure hoping she wouldn't mind doing that considering we just met and all. Years ago Uncle Jesse and I thought it would be fun to just build a log cabin in the woods; so, we began doing that during vacations and getaways where we'd head out here to work on it.

The cabin itself rested two and a half feet off the ground on an already prepared foundation that existed before we commenced building it.

It had five steps leading up to a wraparound porch that had another set in the back. In addition, it also had an easier access to the trail that lead straight to the quarry.

While Lori waited outside for me; I went into grab a bar of soap, two dry towels, and a bottle of shampoo for her.

The inside of the cabin had a small kitchen with naturally a table and chairs, a refrigerator, and a sink.

For our cooking however we'd usually barbecue outside in the back depending on the weather, or if the weather wasn't co-operative we'd cook using the fireplace. In addition, we had us a loft with three beds to sleep which just overlooked the downstairs.

Returning with the things I could think she'd need; I now lead her up to the quarry. Impressed greatly by her stamina I really couldn't help but be as she hardly complained not once about having to walk bare foot over the trails terrain.

"How's your injury doing dose it still hurt?" Walking side by side like we were I felt her warm hand placing itself into mine.

"Pains not so bad really I've felt worse before but thank you Lori for asking though." Seen smiling next at one another we were minutes from breaking through the trees to see the sun's rays hitting its serene setting.

"Oh my it's; its" There as we stepped on to the rock ledge was this secretive hidden paradise of sorts where I spent my summers either swimming; or a lot of times just to come to meditate.

"Gee I never quite had anyone describe it like that exactly; so, I guess you'd like to bath here huh?" Turning with a twinkle in her eye Lori nods her head in immediate approval.

After placing the things down for her I found myself still holding; I respectfully left her there to bath in privacy.

I know your probably thinking to yourself. "Dude are you soft not wanting to watch her bath in the nude." Sure, I could've been like any other pervert and did that of course; but to tell you the truth I wasn't brought up that way.

I was however brought up to respect all people and their individual rights of privacy.

Once up high enough out of sight of her I next removed my shirt; tucking it into a jean belt loop after which I next made myself comfortable on a nearby rock with my legs crossed.

Closing my eyes I began meditating there in this position breathing in slowly; and then exhaling. I had to admit even though my outward appearance might have looked cool as a cucumber; it however was my inner spirit; or Chi I needed to calm.

Sadly my never having a girlfriend bothered me over the years; always training, always competing, and never really having a social life to speak of hurt me deeply. Now however having retired from active competition who knows there just maybe a chance.

Minutes later upon opening my eyes there she was standing there in front of me smiling down upon me now.

Poised like an angel from heaven with the sun perfectly placed behind her head. I continued watching her towel drying her lengthy hair.

"Thank you very much Eddie for suggesting this place to me it's very beautiful here."

"Oh your welcome Lori and yes I agree with you this place is quite beautiful although to tell you the truth this is my first time back here."

"Really? Huh would have imagined you utilizing this place more for bringing your dates to."

"O.K. Well I never actually thought about it like that your right I guess it could've been used for that. Although in all honesty my Uncle wouldn't have approved."

"Wait a minute; let me get this straight then; you mean to tell me I'm the first lady you ever brought up here before?" Sensing quickly an awkward moment was about to occur I exclaimed.

"Well to answer your question; yes, you are the first lady I've brought up here before; but please don't be frightened I'm nothing like your boyfriend or his buddies."

"Boyfriend huh, right Eddie he's my ex-boyfriend thank you very much. Oh and that statement before about me being frightened of you; well I'm not; if anything I'm eternally grateful to you for saving me like you did." Suddenly for some unexpected reason our lips met softly at first as she leaned herself into me.

Personally speaking I never thought in my wildest dreams I'd ever meet anyone as beautiful as Lori-Ann much less be blessed enough to kiss her like I was doing.

Carefully straddling her body on me we continued kissing as I felt her ankles locking behind me. Naturally unsure of what to do next myself; instinctively just let my arms and hands go where they'd feel comfortable.

So, while my right hand placed itself in the small of her back; my left hand however rested itself behind Lori's neck.

But as our kissing intensified our bodies felt an explosion deep within us we couldn't hold back, nor did we really want too.

I remember Uncle Jesse saying to me once. That if your ever lucky enough to find that special someone meant for you. And you feel an explosion deep within you as your kissing her. Then that person is your true love.

Funny thing back then anything Uncle Jesse told me before rarely ever occurred for me…. that is until this very moment.

Now for some strange reason all I really wanted was right here before me. Minutes passed before our lips parted momentarily.

"Are you alright? I'm not too heavy, am I? Oh, how's your pain I'm sorry? Do you want me to get down?" Shrugging her shoulders, a little unsure she keeps smiling at me playfully.

"Yes, I'm all right, No you're not too heavy at all? My pain is fine thanking you for asking; and as far as my wanting you to get down, no I most certainly do not want you to get down thank you." Smiling back at her as our noses slowly touched the others.

"Well that's good you said that you didn't want me to get down; because to tell you the truth I'm quite comfortable." Flashing a bigger grin upon her face over to me.

"All right then I certainly wouldn't want to make you uncomfortable now."

"No you wouldn't want to do that; hey by the way something strange happened when we were kissing before. Like some kind of flame or something igniting inside of me? Laughing out loud to myself my head nods yes back over to her.

"Yes, although I wasn't sure it would ever occur with the two of us kissing however like we were. But trust me it's nothing to worry about, although it does need explaining obviously. And no, it isn't a bad thing, and no it doesn't mean you're going to die or anything." Carefully watching her she continues smiling.

"O.K. So let me see if I got this straight; your telling me that it isn't a bad thing, and it isn't something I'm going to die from, or that I need to worry about, but you can explain it to me; all right then explain it to me."

"Simply put it's our destiny" Pulling back slightly with a half grin upon her face she listens as I explain. "My Uncle Jesse said it to me years ago about this unique thing inside of everyone called "The Burning Flame of Passion.""

"O.K. Well what does this thing do exactly?"

"Believe it or not it doesn't do a thing it lays dormant."

"All right so why is it acting up now when we were kissing then?"

"Uncle Jesse also said to me that if two people happen simply to kiss each other and it ignites within each of them then those two people are destined to be together."

"You know I never really felt this thing happen before with any of my old boyfriends. I mean I've kissed them, but I never felt the kind of wow reaction I felt kissing you."

"The answer to that too is pretty simple; they just weren't the right ones who you were destined to be with that's all plain and simple." As much as I could sense her trying to grasp this unbelievable concept. I felt she needed to be still convinced.

So after gently pulling her back into me I simply kissed her again softly and like earlier our inner flames engulfed each of us simultaneously.

Causing our gentlest of kisses to automatically switch to a much more impassioned one now. Minutes passed before I could be seen carrying her back down to the cabin with my hands beneath her still feeling her soft hands behind my neck. Traditionally after a man and woman meet usually they'd date a while, get to know each other, fall in love through time, and eventually marry, right? Well at least that's the way it goes in real life.

Seen opening the cabin door with my backside; I hit it quickly with my leg to close it. Feeling Lori losing her grip of me; I slowly and gently guide her down until her bare feet touched the soft wooden floor.

"Oh my God; Wow! That was incredible how did you manage to carry me here hurt like you are?" "Well for starters I ignore the pain which again isn't that bad; and basically I just walked carrying you in my arms that's pretty much it."

"Well it was still pretty unbelievable. I like your place here it's cozy."

"Thank you, I like it myself especially for getting away to train and meditate." "So what happens now between us; I mean I'm here with you?"

"Oh right sorry; I forgot to explain what happens next; well according to my Uncle Jesse again he said to me that when two individuals do find one another that their destined to be with each other. They next have to complete this union by performing a very special ceremony between themselves."

Shortly after placing a lit candle down in the middle of the floor I next took Lori's hand walking her over to her spot.

Watching me first sitting down with my legs slightly apart. She next can be seen sitting the same way upon the floor with her legs also slightly apart.

"All right I'll start just watch me." Sensing some nervousness Lori continues watching me closing my eyes taking three deep breaths before saying.

"On this special day Saturday July 4th 1982 I Edward Tyler James do solemnly take you as my wife. I promise to cherish you, honor you, love you, and protect you from harm for the rest of my life, I swear this to you and God." Suddenly my spirit awoke to feeling it tingling inside of me as it next blanketed me.

After that I felt it's calming peace rush over me like warm waters all over my body.

Lowering my head smiling over at Lori-Ann as she smiled back to me watching I see her taking the same deep breaths as I had and next heard her saying.

"On this special Saturday July 4th 1982 I Lori-Ann Wilkerson do solemnly take you as my husband. I promise to cherish you, honor you, love you, and protect you from harm for the rest of my life I swear this to you, and also to God."

Like magic instantly her spirit awoke like mine had done earlier. Although Lori's caused her to giggle as it tickled her still it's calm peace flowed through her like rushing water.

The very last thing we needed to do was kiss, so leaning in as far as we could we kissed sealing our destiny forever. Finally, after blowing out the candle I quickly moved it after that together we happily could be seen consummating our joyful union in the most passioned unbridled. Ah you get the visual of what we're doing.

While other people wouldn't have been able to deal with memories such as these of a loved one who had been abducted. I on the other hand transcended this tragedy into a successful resolve in getting mine back no matter what it took.

The time now as I proceeded outside once more was just after eight o'clock. Our first stop was to check in with Danny.

"Well, where to first big brother?" Asked Elvis watching me pulling out of the driveway. "Thought we'd check in with Danny first to see if his contacts turned up anything." My right foot slid gently off the brake on to the accelerator which catapulted us down the end of the road.

It felt like there was less humidity today than yesterday as we hit the expressway.

Meanwhile back at police headquarters B.J. and Uncle Jesse had gotten the report back from forensics confirming their suspicions about the second voice and just who it belonged to. But as B.J. was in the process of getting a copy of that report to bring us up to speed on what he un-covered.

Elvis and I were just getting out of my car behind the Black Dragon Restaurant; the time now was 8:45a.m. After entering we began ascending the stairs up to the rooms; Danny's was the fifth room on the right.

There were ten rooms in all on the floor above the restaurant that Sue rented out. It also had a bathroom and a shower room with two shower heads.

It didn't take long before Danny answered my knock upon his door before we were allowed to enter into his room.

"Good Morning guy's thanks for coming over; Hey Eddie got some news for you about your cousin's co-worker there: seems like Agent Givens got himself re-assigned up to Lemmington Vermont."

It wouldn't be until our host made us a couple cups of coffee; before we could all be seen taking our seats.

"Lemmington Vermont huh, talk about a coincidence." "Wonder what he's doing up there?"

"Sorry Elvis my source couldn't tell me that; but hey Eddie, I did manage to find this on my lap top; seems like your buddy Kenny Stevenson got himself replaced as sheriff up there."

"Replaced how?"

"According to the web page he was caught in his motel room with two chicks." Bringing up the page for us we examined it for ourselves right there.

"According to this his resignation was immediate pending a special independent investigation of the charges against him; and guess who the lead investigator is?"

"Don't tell me big brother; ah Special Agent Jerome Givens." "Bingo; little brother you got it."

"Well so much for it being a fair investigation with him leading it."

It certainly didn't take but listening to my reaction a while ago about Kenny's dismissal as Lemmington's sheriff. Before Elvis could almost sense himself, a road trip was clearly in the works for all of us.

(First time I met Kenny was 1974 while visiting the small town I see this young deputy getting thrown out of a salon.

"You ok. Deputy?"

"Yeah, thanks for catching me; man, those three are really busting up the place.' "You got any back-up?'

No it's just me, the sheriff is drunk back at the office.' Extending my hand to him I helped him up. "Tell you what I'll be your back-up; let's go." As we both entered the establishment I caught the first guy trying to punch me, grabbing his arm I twisted it quick tossing his ass over the bar hard.

The deputy tried jumping on the back of his man trying his best to get his arm around his neck to force him down, hitting his man with a beer bottle knocking him out the deputy fell on top of the second guy.

The third man tried charging us I simply lifted my leg kicking the guy knocking him out.

After helping the young deputy secure the hell raisers he smiles holding out his hand to me.

"My name's Kenny Stevenson appreciate your assistance here." Shaking it firmly back I exclaimed back. "Pleasure to meet you Kenny; my name's Eddie James." His eyes widened as he exclaimed back. "Whoa you mean the martial arts champion? I saw your last fight up in NH." The long and the short of it ever since that first meeting we've been friends ever since.

But before any road trip could be considered we needed to re-confirm this information we had gotten before making the four-hour trek up there.

The time now was just after nine o'clock while we waited for Danny to get himself dressed and ready to re-open the restaurant downstairs.

Minutes passed before the three of us could be seen descending the stairs together.

Seeing Snake and B.J. Entering next; the four of us begin assisting Danny in opening the restaurant. "Great seeing you guys here; saves me a dime; got some more information,"

"Really cuz; well isn't that a coincidence so have we." By the time we had gotten the chairs down off the tables the rest of Danny's crew had since arrived.

The time now was just after ten o'clock when we all could seen grabbing a table in the back of the restaurant.

"Witnessed Agent Givens about one thirty in the morning leaving his house with his bags packed." Snake exclaims first to us.

"Well that pretty much confirms the phone conversation I had taped earlier this morning between him and McKenna." Pausing we listened as B.J. Explained staking out his former boss's house where he happened to tape two very interesting phone conversations.

The first tape was of Givens, and McKenna discussing first of all things Kenny's dismissal as sheriff.

And then Jerome asked his boss if he got paid; which McKenna replied yes, he had.

Not until B.J. played the second tape that he then told the rest of us about the muffled voice we were hearing belonged to none other than Maxwell Escabar.

"So McKenna and Escabar are in this together interesting; my guess is Givens must have been recruited around the same time as you had begun poking around trying to dig up anything on Escabar." Watching him nodding his head to us listening they hear me exclaim.

"Something also is nagging in my gut; that suggests my friend Sheriff Kenny Stevenson met up with the very same circumstance as you cousin being set-up."

"So I guess this means we take this investigation on the road huh?" Seeing the others nodding their heads in confirmation to being on board left me lastly nodding mine to re-confirm that indeed was our next plan.

The time now was just after eleven o' clock, as we left the restaurant together. It suddenly became apparent that I had no idea what we were going up against. So, I teamed B.J. and Snake up to get us whatever special supplies they could think of that we might be needing.

Leaving my brother and I at the house to get ourselves prepared.

But while team James was preparing for its future venture up toward the northern Vermont town Meanwhile Maxwell Escabar however was carefully observing the selection process of his slaves there before him in his throne room by his men.

With Brenda standing just to his left; and Lori-Ann positioned to his right. The three smiled as they continue watching the proceedings.

As each victim is selected they are next escorted out of the throne room; and into another preparation room.

Where they are completely brain washed after which they are re-programed into full-time erotic tickle slaves to their newest Mistress; and her name is Mistress Katrina.

Deep within her hidden underground bordello she along with her associates further torture their victims in order to re-sell them to their clients. Who yearns just to own a slave for their ticklish pleasure.

It's still hard to imagine that there were truly others out there beyond the U.S boarders. With this secret fascination to tickle helpless women in tight restraints and willing to pay any price to obtain such victims as these.

As his right-hand man can be seen climbing the steps Maxwell Escabar smiles more as his man next hands him a clipboard for his inspection

"Ah I see you've completed your task Alexander excellent; Well even though we maybe loosing these slaves to Mistress Katrina, we will be three quarters of a million dollars richer." Smiling back; Alexander having saw his master was indeed pleased nodded his head as he went back to continue his work on the before mentioned selected slaves.

The new room all of the slaves found themselves seated in could best be described as a collage lecture hall with a strange area in closed directly below them with a control board. Upon each of their heads was a virtual reality helmet where images of each of their separate lives were at that moment being slowly erased before them. Minutes passed by the time Alexander could be seen next entering much to his delight he had arrived just in time to view the slaves now being re-programed into their final stages as erotic tickle slaves.

But as the three hundred or so slaves continued having their minds altered.

Back at the house however Snake and B.J. Returned to help my brother and I in our preparation to the small town of Lemmington Vermont. The time now was 1:30PM.

"Jesus cuz, we have enough hardware here to start our own war."

"Let's just hope it doesn't come down to that B.J. But yeah I'd say we are fully stocked" "I'll say: Hey excuse me for asking, but just where will we be setting up camp?"

"Don't sweat it B.J. I got that covered." Replied Elvis to the rest of us. With B.J. Riding with Snake; Elvis and I could be seen taking the lead thus beginning our journey.

I drove my customized van while Elvis checked the map and navigated. Sure felt good having him along riding shotgun beside me. It was another hazy, hot, and humid day with the temperature expected to hit 89 degrees today.

Watching him getting up carefully he reaches behind me and into my small cooler to get us two bottles of water putting one beside me.

"Going to be another New England scorcher today." Smiling nodding my head to him. Together we watched the traffic passing us seeing a Johnsburry truck passing us listening to hear it beeping at us as it passed us.

"Excuse me Elvis for asking this; but what did you mean before when you told B.J. Not to sweat where will we be setting up camp at I mean is there something you're not telling me?" Wishing the hell, I knew more about him since our reunion the other day after twenty years. *(All I really could remember was just watching him at the airport about to board a private plane with Mr. Jacob Daniel's an old army friend of Uncle Jesse's Who said that he could help my brother to come to terms with the tragedy of our parent's car explosion, so he went to live with Mr. Daniel's down in the Louisiana Bayou.)*

I could see him hesitating momentarily before exclaiming back.

"Guess it's time for me to come clean big brother, but do me a favor just don't get overly excited about what I'm about to tell you." Seen nodding head it signaled Elvis that I silently promised him not to get overly excited about what he was about to divulge to me.

"All right before you go hearing it from anyone else; I have to confess that my net worth is about ten million dollars and some change." My jaw instantly dropped after listening to that, but without a reply back from me Elvis continued speaking.

"Sorry Eddie for shocking you like that, but believe me if I could have confessed that any sooner to you I would've." Seconds passed as my mouth finally closed before I exclaimed back.

"Gee Elvis, I'm proud of you, but just how did you come into acquire this money?"

"Well it was after I left Mr. Daniel's in 1977; that I began trekking cross country. I picked up odd jobs here and there until July of that year. When I became employed as an assistant to Clinton Tucker a Wall St Tycoon who made his first million dollars at the age of 21."

"I read about him in the papers; wow good for you Elvis so what did you do for him exactly?"

"Pretty much anything he needed to do for him. But mostly he hired me as a sounding board or so he said. He explained to me that he needed someone who could just listen to him; and at times offer my advice to him. Without sounding like a yes man which, he then said to me he already plenty of those."

"I can imagine he did. Well that's great Elvis; so how long were you employed by him?" "Eight years Eddie; he passed away in his sleep in the spring of 1985."

"Sorry to hear that Elvis."

"Yeah thanks big brother, at the reading of his will I was almost as shocked as you were when I heard Mr. Tucker included me in his will to the tune of ten million dollars for my loyal service to him."

"Ah, so that's how you came into that money huh, well I'm proud of you bro."

The time now was a little after 5:00P.M When we saw ourselves rolling in through the small town.

It resembled an old west town with its wooden sidewalks in front of the buildings that were there.

It had its Sheriff office, a bank, a general store, and a saloon according to Elvis it also had rooms to rent just over the establishment also. Its dirt roads felt weird underneath us as we rolled slowly through.

Finally parking behind what looked like a rear entrance we all could be seen getting out following my brother as he leads the way inside.

"Hope you guys are hungry?" Elvis exclaimed looking back at us.

It wouldn't be until opening the inner door that we could see a full working kitchen with workers hustling to complete orders right before us.

"Elvis is this someone's restaurant?" I asked him.

"It's a retro pub big brother; with as you can see a kitchen, but if you'll follow me I want to check out the crowed we have tonight."

Smiling we followed him through the kitchen and out to the front where we could see indeed it was crowded with people socializing and having a good time. Some could be seen dancing on its dance floor, while others dinned, and for those who just wanted to meet this place also had a fully stocked bar.

Pulling Elvis aside I next could be heard exclaiming. "All right Elvis we can see this place is packed, but just what aren't you telling us?" But just before answering me a waitress kind of answered my question for me when she exclaimed.

"Hi Boss welcome back we missed you." Turning toward us, we could see him smiling at us as he replied.

"Guess Veronica spilled the beans its true this is my place, I call it Flashback."

One of the perks of being out of the public eye was not being recognized at first for having been a five-time martial arts champion. Naturally of course there were those fans who did fondly remember my matches.

The time now was around 5:30P.M. When we could be seen making our way up to the second floor. Exactly like on the lower level this also had a dance area, and bar. But as the four of us could be seen being seated on the upper level of the pub.

The three hundred slaves having already been bought and paid for by Mistress Katrina were slowly walking up the three metal ramps and into the three separate tractor trailer trucks, at that very moment.

Carefully monitoring the proceedings from within his underground office was Escabar.. Smiling to himself he re-confirms the three quarter of a million dollar transaction he received from the Singaporean Mistress.

Several minutes passed as Escabar smiled; seeing the very last of his former slaves stepping carefully into the trucks.

Seated behind him tightly restrained inside of two separate 18th century wrist, ankle, and head stocks were Brenda as well as Lori-Ann.

Seen with their heads lowered the two hooded damsels quickly awaken after hearing the fingers of their demented Master snapping. But unable to voice their displeasure over what was about to happen to them.

Unzipping their mouth listening he hears both ladies there before him laughing hysterically. As Lori and Brenda felt the fingers vibrating being felt on the soles of both their feet.

"That's right ladies; laugh your asses off for me; come on this is a celebration my lovelies, so let's celebrate; shall we?" Turning he catches site of the very last truck pulling away from the mountain side with its most valuable of cargo.

But as Maxwell Escabar was continuing to celebrate with his two personal slaves there in his secret control room.

CHAPTER SEVEN

"Well Kenny now that you're on board; I think it's time to show my brother and everyone the operation huh?" Exclaimed Elvis with a wink in his eye to Kenny. Shortly after we followed them back down to the first level again.

"Elvis just what operation are you taking about?" I asked him as we watched him reaching behind the cash register to press what looked like a hidden button.

Which it then opened up the floor behind the bar to expose a series of stairs leading downward. "Come on big brother I'll explain just what I'm talking about."

As Kenny and my brother lead the way down, Snake, B.J. and I followed without much of a choice in the matter.

Noticing dim lights as we neared the bottom we were all suspicious as to just what we were to encounter at the bottom of the steps. Putting those suspicions to rest by the time we had the three of us were amazed at a secret hidden underground network of martial artists.

"Well Eddie this is the last of the surprises I'd like to give you a tour of my secret operation here."

As Elvis began showing us the things around us I for the first time in my life was truly impressed. "I bet your wondering just why I do have this set-up and it can be easily explained."

"When I first came to Lemmington years ago the town was in turmoil. With prostitution, drugs, and corruption running ramped; the long and the short of it.

There were others who felt as I did, so little by little we cleaned up the town. By getting rid of the drug pushers, as well as the corrupt town officials.

As for the prostitutes I gave them a choice; if they cleaned up their act they could work for me legitimately as waitresses, so they did. Seen smiling toward him I couldn't help but imagine what it took to get this operation started. but couldn't have been prouder either in just what he has accomplished.

"What can I say Little brother; you saw a bad situation and with the help of your friends made it much better I'm proud of you."

"Thanks Eddie I appreciate the compliment; so, don't my guys here who I couldn't have done this without them." As Elvis continued his tour we saw five to six shower rooms, and locker rooms. We also saw five to six dojos' down there as well with instructors teaching classes in self-defense from beginners to advanced.

Better-man, see you finally packed on some muscle after this many years about time." Seeing another old friend of mine jogging over to me we shook hands then hugged each other. "Christ Eddie it's been years how've you been?"

"Been better but hanging in there, it's good seeing you here. my kid brother treating you good?" "Hell yeah, I'm a sense here; teaching these younger kids how it's done the right way." "They look like a good eager group."

"They are great students, hey don't mean to cut this short but I need to head back it's good seeing you again." After tapping me on the shoulder playfully. Ricky jogs back to resume his class before his students cool down.

Thinking back I first met Ricky Better-man back in 1975 after a match he had to win his second black belt. We kind of bumped into each other and have been friends ever since.

"Thought you got lost big brother."

"No Elvis just saying hello to one of your instructors…Ricky Better-man he and I go back a way's." Grinning we walk away to rejoin the others.)

Not meaning to draw attention to myself I couldn't help but pause in the doorways of a couple of those classes to look in. Which resulted in me signing a couple of autographs, and meeting those students who spotted me standing there.

Our tour continued with my brother's war room with its series of monitors his men kept a watchful eye on everything.

"Hope you guys don't think I'm a pervert with this part of my operation; but I just need to make sure we have evidence of a felony or a mister meaner being committed before my guys respond to anything suspicious." Have to admit my brother still impressed me. Watching the various monitors showing us natural settings of people doing their jobs within town.

"In addition to my men I also have these six ladies monitoring the communications as well for anything suspicious that might be said to anyone we don't know about." Elvis exclaimed to us stepping back after patting those ladies on the shoulders which they responded by smiling back toward him.

"Speaking of anyone you should know about Elvis has that piss ant Jerome Givens been communicating with anybody suspicious since he arrived here?"

"As a matter of fact big brother he has but whoever he is communicating with has some sort of voice distorted or something to make the other persons voice unrecognizable." Stepping forward B.J. could be seen placing a cassette tape into a recorder for everyone to hear garbled, then he next replaces with another tape un-garbled.

"Don't sweat it Elvis I have something in my bag of tricks here you can hook up to your communications that will make any future conversation Jerome has clear as a bell with who-ever he's talking with." Remembering his shopping experience from earlier there was one apparatus he had brought with him for just this special occasion.

So while B.J. went to get his special toy to install; Snake and I decided to go checkout the goings on at the sheriff's office.

I knew my brother's underground network was something for him to be proud of. But unfortunately, it lacked the up close and personal touch as getting into the town itself and questioning folks on just what they knew or didn't know.

While Snake spoke with those shopkeepers on their personal takes on their newly elected sheriff and his associate.

I on the hand proceeded into the den of the monster himself just to see if I could rattle his cage just a bit.

"Well, Well, Well, if it isn't Eddie James aren't you a little bit off your turf here?" Asked Givens in his smuggest of voices.

"Not really agent Givens I go to where the clues lead me; but I could ask you the same thing what brings you up here?" Knowing my reply could have been construed as instigating in nature; I still awaited Givens response to it.

"Not that it's any of your business, but my boss decided to reassign me here."

"Ah I see; well I'm sure Tex knows what he is doing; but I just think it's funny why a top F.B.I. agent like yourself would ever consider coming to this town of all places?"

Smiling to myself I could sense his smugness starting to turn into pure frustration, as I continued standing there awaiting another response from him.

"Again Mr. James not that it's any of your business but I don't question my boss's decisions he makes in re-assigning me here of all places."

"I do however consider it an honor to be considered a top dog around here with absolutely no one to answer too." Though he may have been right he certainly didn't have anyone to answer too. But as I was about to leave him I did however leave him with a final thought to gnaw on.

"Think you may be right Givens it might not be any of my business nor is it my place to second guess your boss's decision on your re-assignment here for you."

"But can I leave you with a little piece of advice. Never self-proclaim to anyone it's an honor for you to be considered a top dog, Because I've got a news flash for you; right now, there's a new top dog in town." And with that having been said I slowly backed out of the sheriff's office not once taking my eyes off him.

The time now was 7:45PM With our initial questioning of certain individuals within the town having been achieved Snake and I met back at the van to return to the others back at the pub

"How did your meeting go with Givens?" Asked Snake as he watched me turning the van around to leave.

"As well as could be expected; he was surprised to see me here; as I was to see him." I replied back to him; as the van began slowly pulling away.

"I bet, did he tell you why he was here?"

"Ah Huh, he said that his boss re-assigned him here of all places which I questioned then was told it was none of my business; but then he considered it an honor being catch this a top dog." Looking over to see Snake smiling he next replied back.

"In the words of your cousin; "Oh Boy" well just what did you say back when he declared that to you?" Smiling back myself watching him out of the corner of my eye I said back.

Oh, Snake you would have been proud of me because I just declared back to him that he shouldn't be calling himself a top dog because there was a new dog in town now. After which I left him there." Laughing together Snake next replied by saying.

"Bet he appreciated that burr you stuck him with huh?" Nodding my head still with a smile upon my face I said back. "Let's just see how long it takes him to dig that deep one out because I buried it good." But as Snake was in the process of telling what he found out after talking with the shopkeepers.

Blocking the road just ahead of my van was a welcoming committee of sorts. Two pick-up trucks parked themselves sideways blocking either access on both sides of the road, and with me in my van; I wasn't exactly ready to be in need of body work on it anytime soon, so we slowed to a stop there just ahead of them.

"Guess these are the ones Givens must have called to help him get that burr out of his ass?" I replied over toward Snake who was doing as I was; calculating just how many they were.

"I count 14 dose that compute with you too?"

"That's a Rodger on that I got 14 counted too; 7 in the left truck; and 7 in the right truck. Guess we should get out and see what the problem is?" Answering back as we next got out of the van.

"Good evening gentlemen can my friend and I assist you in giving you directions to the S/M party you're looking for?" I replied over to the first man dressed as his friends were in black leather shorts, with matching leather boots, and chains criss crossed up their chests and down their backs.

"Cute Mr. James, but you see it's you and your friend who are mistaken if you think we need the help; on the contrary. It's my men and I who'll be assisting you to get out and back to Boston where you belong while you still can."

"Oh really; Well thanks for this tip; my friend and I appreciate it, but were not getting out, or for that matter going back to Boston.; Besides since you brought it up. How did you know we were from Boston?" Together Snake and I looked to one another perplexed to his knowing that about us.

Sad as it was to see from our vantage point, as his men kept coming at us one by one the harder and even more quicker did they get themselves knocked out.

Courtesy of us of course; until only the one who informed us to get out before was the last of them standing amongst those who had falling there before Snake and I. After grabbing him then throwing him back against the side of one of those trucks did I reply back.

"Now I'd like to inform you on just what you're going to be doing. First you're going to pick up your girlfriends here and get the hell out of my sight. Because if my friend and I see you or your goof troop here will be finishing what we started that's a fact.

Oh, and when you see your wimp of a boss give him a message for me. Tell him if he grows himself a set of balls and wants some to come get some and we'll be more than happy to kick his chicken shit ass too." Together Snake and I starred this loud-mouthed hooligan down as we left him there to tend to his fallen friends.

"You don't think that had anything to do with your meeting earlier with Agent Givens, or not?" Asked Snake as we could be seen walking back to the van.

"Can't say for sure Snake it very well could've been. Or it could've been a scare tactic of some kind just to see if we'd be spooked in any way. But all I am sure about is we certainly did get someone's attention tonight." Nodding his head in silent agreement.

We Carefully watched those who we had fought slowly getting themselves back up off the ground there in front of us.

Meanwhile back at the pub one of the ladies monitoring the communications was at that moment switching on the recorder to tape the following phone conversation for everyone there to hear.

"Agent Givens? What are you calling me for now?"

"Sorry boss to bother you, but your friend's men couldn't stop him."

"Jesus Christ man what do you expect me to do from here?"

"A little advice wouldn't hurt sir about now; I mean even you have to admit sir dealing with this one isn't as easy as his cousin was in setting him up at F.B.I. Headquarters."

"Yes, you're absolutely right about that listen you caught me in something I'm finishing up call me back in thirty minutes and I'll have some advice to give you on what you can do about him." Switching off the recorder the young lady smiles as Elvis pats her on the shoulder to signal a job well done on her part.

"Well B.J. Guess that taped confession by Givens clears you in the eyes of the law."

"Yeah now all we need is for a judge to hear it; I knew that little snot set me up with those drugs." Taking his fist hitting it into his opposite opened hand B.J. Next nods his head towered Elvis who nods his back.

Thinking back to what I had previously said to that man; though I might not have been wrong. When I made the remark to him about his boss needing to grow a new set of balls; however. I was when I replied to him that if his boss wanted some to come get some and we'll be more than happy to kick his chicken shit ass too. Even though I may have been aggravated enough over getting ambushed by those men before. I certainly should have known better to have mouthed off like that. Being a martial artist like I was still didn't give me the right to sound off offensive and threating like that.

"Still thinking about your statement you made to that guy earlier?" Snake asked watching me drive. "Yes, sorry about that old friend; I should've known better before opening my mouth like that." "Forget it Eddie, you certainly wouldn't be human if you didn't have that emotion running thru you. And besides I have to admire you for holding it together up until that point, so you really don't have to apologize for that."

"Thanks Snake I appreciate you understanding like that; now I just have to put that episode behind me; and refocus it on the case so what if anything did the shopkeepers tell you?"

Listening to hear from Snake that everyone he had questioned wasn't too impressed with their newest so called sheriff brought a much welcomed smile to my face. It also suggested that it was only a matter of time before Special Agent Givens would be himself on the opposite side of the law.

The time now as we arrived back at my brother's pub was 8:45p.m. We immediately brought Kenny, Elvis, and B.J. up to date on our two encounters.

After which Snake and I listened to the previous phone conversation between Givens and McKenna that brought another smile on my face.

"Congratulations B.J. that pretty much seals you getting back with the bureau after a judge hears that confession by Givens." I said smiling over toward him.

"Yeah cuz, looks that way, but hey now what's on the agenda?"

"Glad you asked me; I was thinking of monitoring the rest of tonight's communications. Then in the morning taking that recording you taped at McKenna's house then really seeing if we can make Agent Givens squirm."

Watching B.J. Rubbing his hands together like he was with an evil smile upon his face. Suggested to me that B.J. Was indeed eager to reacquaint himself with his old colleague once more.

The time now was 9:00p.m. When Givens could be heard dialing the phone in the sheriff's office.

"Tex? It's Jerome can you talk now?"

"Yes, now I can."

"Sorry about before boss about contacting you."

"Forget it Givens, so what did Eddie say to you upon seeing you there?" "Just that he thought it was strange seeing me reassigned here of all places." "And what did you say back to him?"

"That it was none of his business and then I reminded him that there was a new dog in town."

"Excellent; if he persists tell him if he doesn't back off that you'll have charges brought up against him on obstruction of justice that should back him off."

"I don't know if that will work, but I'll try?"

"Try? You better do more than try Agent Givens; you'd better be dam well convincing." With that having been said Tex hung up his phone ahead of Agent Givens.

Taking this tape out then marking it I placed it with the others. "Have to love Tex and Jerome with these conversations back n forth to each other. They're really digging a deep hole for themselves."

"Uncle Jesse used to say to me long time ago just be patient enough. With an investigation then give a suspect a little rope. And eventually they'll hang themselves with it."

While Snake was outside doing his type of monitoring from the shadows of the night for anything or anyone suspicious.

"Think Snake's having any luck?" Asked Elvis handing me a cup of coffee.

"Hard to say for sure Little brother. But knowing Snake like I do; I'm sure if he did find anything we would've heard from him by now."

"That's true; sorry I'm just." Dropping his head to his chest I next replied back.

"I know little brother; I know." I could sense Elvis was anxious about getting more involved with this case, but for now all we could do was patiently wait.

Speaking of Snake however he indeed was taken every advantage of his ninja skills to try and produce something in a lead for us.

Sneaking up to overhear two men talking about just coming back from the docks in Boston after completing a transfer of three large storage containers.

Peaked my friends interest so much that not only did he place a bug into their trucks cell phones.

But also, a couple microscopic camera bugs as well in and around the cabs of their trucks.

"Attention, Attention this goes out to my party who's listening out there; looking for the baddest of bad guy's. Come back come back?"

"We hear you Snake; what you got over?"

"I caught up with two of them punks we had a run in with earlier remember Eddie?" "How could I forget them; yeah I remember."

"All right then; turn up your receivers. And switch on whatever monitor you have available there to see where I'm transmitting from?" Quickly Elvis switches on the new monitor to view Snake standing just behind an empty tractor.

"O.K. Snake we see you." I said watching him there.

"Good; I placed two camera bugs on this truck and the one next to it; I also bugged there cells as well so not only do we have site, but we have sound over."

"Great work Snake head on back before you're spotted." Know that was a rhetorical quote on my part got my blood brother laughing to himself as he next replied back.

"Eddie, you of all people should know I may see whoever I'm looking at; but they never in their wildest dreams can ever see me."

Upon completing his statement Snake next could be seen disappearing in a puff of smoke. Minutes pass before the two men return to their rigs unknown that they were being watched and listened to on the James boy network.

"Recognize the place their pulling away from Elvis?"

"Think so; looks like the diner off Route3 near Maidstone." Going over to the map I place a colored pin near that.

"Should be traveling through town or past it within I'd guess 45 minutes to an hours' time wouldn't you think?"

"That sounds about right to me big brother." Replied Elvis back over to me.

"Now comes the tricky part scrambling your men to various areas along this route to watch for them." "Ah I'd hate to sound like a kill joy Eddie, but I think you better come over here and check this out first?"

There on the monitor my brother and I see both rigs vanish from our site.

"What the? How could they disappear like that?"

"Here put this on Elvis; there they are see?" It wouldn't be until putting on a pair of inferred glasses that we indeed saw them once more.

"I don't get it; what do they have some kind of cloaking device or something?"

"Exactly Yes Elvis that's what it is." There in front of us on the monitor all we could see was the red off their heated bodies still within those rig cabs.

"Snake; you got them?"

"That's a rodger Eddie; I'm right behind them."

"Keep your eye on the monitor and I'll get back to you on where to roundevue with me; Snake out." Having said that Elvis and I continued watching the monitor and Snake tailing them. The time now was 2:00a.m. As we Maintained our constant visual hoping it wouldn't end in another dead end. Maxwell Escabar however was continuing his; from his observation room as his newest delivery of slaves could all be seen seated with not only their legs straight out in front of them. But upon each of their heads were virtual reality helmets on all being brainwashed there before him.

"This batch however will only be brainwashed after which they'll be held on standby for the newest client who might be in need of an immediate shipment." Another evil smile could be seen upon his face as he continues watching the proceedings.

Elvis and I however were finding ourselves being relieved by Kenny and B.J. Who were next brought up to speed on the latest developments concerning Snake and just who he was tailing.

"That's great well hopefully those two boobs will lead us to Escabar." Said B.J. looking up at the monitor.

"We can only hope cuz." I exclaimed back as my brother and I could be seen leaving the room.

Sadly, for the rest of the night we heard nothing in the way of results coming out of the war room. No communications were being transmitted and no word from Snake either on the trailing of the two suspects it was like he just disappeared.

Meanwhile deep below Sable mountain the two drivers were now pulling their rigs up to an appreciative Maxwell Escabar for another job successfully done.

"Congratulations Gentlemen I take it you had no problems?" Asked Escabar.

"No problems master in getting there or dropping off the cargo to the storage containers. We watched them being loaded on to the ship, then left after that. But we did pick up a tail following us after leaving a diner we stopped at coming back from the docks, but were happy to report we lost him before coming back here." Replied one of the drivers back to him.

"Excellent, well go get some sleep; because you have another delivery in a few hours. I'll have somebody sweep your vehicles just in case." Said Escabar to the drivers who were now walking past him.

But as Escabar stood there watching them walking he produces a 45. Caliber revolver after which he then shoots both men in the head.

The hours passed swiftly for us; the time now was 5:00a.m. As we woke to another day. My brother and I still hadn't heard anything from Snake on his two suspects he had been tailing; that of course until we had gotten ourselves outside to do our pre-stretch before our run.

"Lookie here, Lookie here, Lookie here, this here is the third driver who wasn't at the diner with his two buddies who gave him the slip." Together the three of us brought the still unconscious driver into the pub..

By the time we had; we were joined by Kenny and B.J. "Who's this?"

Asked B.J. With a puzzled look upon his face after which I explained just who he was. "Really? Well talk about catching a break huh?"

"Yeah; now all we have to do is hope he wakes up, so we can question him."

"Think I have that covered Eddie." Reaching into his pocket Snake next produces a vile of smelling salts swiping it a couple of times under the man's nose he begins to stir waking up.

"Where? Where am I?" Asked the young man sitting up more in his chair.

"Never mind where you are; just answer some questions I have for you and we won't hurt you." I said kneeling down in front of him.

"All right let's start with something simple like what's your name for starters?" "Jake"

"All right see how easy that was Jake; My name's Eddie, this here to your right is my cousin Robert, and to your left is my brother Elvis; Snake you already know he's my blood brother and this gentleman here is sheriff Kenny Stevenson." Uncle Jesse taught me that if you ever wanted to get a suspect to talk about what he knew your best bet was to always be polite.

Seeing his tension easing after shaking everyone's hands in meeting them I next asked.

"Now Jake I'd like to know where you were coming back from in your rig when Snake stopped you." Hesitant at first it took Jake several minutes after getting his head together before he replied.

"I was coming back from the docks in Boston; Pierre 44 my friends and I were there to un-load our trailers into three separate storage containers. Which took 90 minutes to complete; after that we were told to unhook our trailers and drive away, so that's what we did." Most of the time a person's facial expression will lead that individual to lie; but Snake and I could tell by Jake's that he was telling us the truth.

"See here; I have the copy of the purchaser's invoice; one of the dock workers handed it to me upon our leaving." Sure, enough as I took it from him it most definitely was a purchaser's invoice.

CHAPTER EIGHT

Taken a moment before continuing my questioning of Jake; and what he may have known I stopped long enough together with the others to examine that purchase invoice.

"Boston Harbor; Dock 38: Pierre; 44 Departure time; 12: 00a.m Figures this doesn't say who the purchaser is, but it does say here whatever this ship is carrying it's 300 units. Hey Jake what's this 300 units mean?" At first Jake's hesitation could've been warranted given the fact he was unconscious when he arrived but as he continued to sit there in silence stalling for time now.

"Come on Jake your dong good; don't quit on us what does this 300 units mean?" I wasn't sure if he was doing this deliberately or if he was under orders from Escabar. But he maintained his right to remain silent as we continued sitting there.

"Great now that we have someone to question he decides to go silent." Replies B.J. Back over to us. "Listen Jake; I don't know if you're aware of this or not, but Maxwell Escabar the man you're working for is a stone-cold killer. Who murdered our parents in a car bombing across the street from our house when my brother and I were kids. But maybe you're thinking to yourself I'm making this all up; well think long and hard on it because it's fact.

Another fact that I should enlighten you on is kidnapping is a felony and false imprisonment yep that's a felony too, so you think about that while your remaining silent like you are, or if you'd rather not spend the rest of your life in prison with him inside the same cell. I'd highly suggest you tell us everything you know starting with these 300 units and what it means?"

Watching him swallowing hard I certainly hope I gave him something to consider.

Minutes passed however before he exclaimed. "The term units are a special code we use it means slaves." "So, if anybody reads it; it's just 300 units, but you and your associates it's read 300 slaves clever." "Well now that we got you back with us talking where were these slaves being shipped too?"

"A secret port in Singapore where Mistress Katrina was to be signing for them upon their delivery." "And how much is Escabar getting for these slaves?"

"Has gotten all ready actually; he already has three hundred thousand dollars pre-paid to him." "I see, so is my brother's fiancé and my wife part of this shipment to Singapore per-chance?" "No, they're not; Escabar has them near to him; almost everywhere he goes.

"He refers to them as his pleasure toys" Out of frustration we all watched as Elvis could be seen throwing a chair clear across the room in anger over listening to this.

"Excuse me a minute Jake." Grabbing Elvis by the arm I ushered him out of range; and beside the bar to exclaim.

"Elvis listen to me; I'm not going to correct you on what you did throwing that chair like that; God knows I wanted to also, but we can't loose our cool not when we got him talking." Watching him with his head lowered I listened as he replied back. "Sorry Eddie your right I almost blew it there for you; Arrg! I'm so so." Nodding my head back toward him I sympathized with just how frustrated he might have been.

Seeing Kenny walking over toward us we next listen as he exclaims. "I don't know if that was a scripted bit you two worked out amongst yourselves but congratulations; you got him talking; he's over there spilling his guts to B.J. and Snake as we speak." It wouldn't be until receiving a play full thumbs up from Snake that we next smiled looking over to him returning his attention back to Jake.

Covering a broad scope of topics asked by B.J. Jake's answers ranged from Escabar's escape from Bellevue; to his first abductions back in the summer of 1987 in California; to enlisting the aid of Tex McKenna just to keep any of the various authorities from digging too deep in finding him.

Jake also in interviewing him confirmed that Agent Givens had been responsible for getting our cousin fired from the bureau by planting himself those two small baggies of cocaine in not only his personal locker; but also in his gym locker as well.

Promising Jake to put him into protective custody I turned him over to Kenny who next could be seen escorted him down behind the bar to Elvis's underground hideaway.

The time now 6:40a.m. Though I might have wanted to bring him I asked Elvis if he wouldn't mind staying here until we got back from making Jerome squirm with that special cassette of B. J's. Seeing him smiling back at us he then agreed to keep an extra eye on Jake while we were gone.

Minutes passed before B.J. And I could be seen leaving Flashback together.

"You do have a plan?"

"Yep I do Cuz; I'm going into the sheriff's office through the front." "All right that sounds good for you; but what exactly will I be doing?"

"Oh, you'll be coming into the sheriff's office through the back door though; after giving me five minutes inside to play that cassette tape you recorded of McKenna and him."

"So if he decides to make a run for it I'll be covering the rear of the office to prevent his escaping clever cuz." "Thanks; I thought you'd like that; All right; let's see the cassette player; Tapes rewound and in there good; Here is a walkie talkie when you get in position back their key it quickly two times. Then wait five minutes after that then stroll in the back got it?"

"Got it; Give me a minute." Nodding my head, I next watched him carefully getting into position.

After signaling me with the keys from his walkie talkie it was now officially 7:10a.m.

It certainly may not have looked like him doing paper work, but that's just what he was doing as I strolled into Kenny's office.

"Look at you doing paper work trying to play the role of a small-town sheriff; sorry to be the one to inform you Jerome, but Lemmington already has an honest man for that job which unfortunately puts you out." I exclaimed in a serious voice.

"Listen Eddie; I hate to burst your bubble, but I'm in charge of this office now. Oh and I spoke with my boss Tex McKenna and he has a message for you. He says that if you don't stop poking your nose where it doesn't belong he'll have you brought up on charges of interfering with a federal investigation." Agent Givens replied back still seated behind Kenny's desk.

"Oh really he said that huh? Well let's just hope were cell mates huh? Pulling out the recorder I quickly pushed play playing the conversation between him and Tex McKenna days ago outside of Tex McKenna's house. After which I next could be seen stopping it.

"So tell me what part of a federal investigation dose setting up a local sheriff fall under? Or for that matter interfering with another colleges investigation by setting him up with two small baggies of cocaine. An illegal substance I might add that you were in the possession of prior to that little shared at F.B.I. Headquarters who orchestrated that I wonder?" Stepping back now from the desk I continued watching him unable to answer with his quick wit or his smugness.

After picking up my recorder then placing it back into my pocket we listen to hear the back door open where next to enter through it was none other than B.J. "Hey Cuz It's good seeing you."

"Thanks Eddie it's good seeing you too."

"Jerome? Hi, remember me the guy you set up I certainly have been biting my time hoping to run into you again, so has he said anything yet Eddie?"

"No Sorry Cuz he hasn't"

"Really? Well you mind if I try to get him to talk." Watching B.J. Pulling out a 38. Caliber revolver we next watch him emptying it only to replace it with one single bullet spinning the chambers next.

"What? What is he doing?" Asked Agent Givens watching B.J. walking up to him.

"Not sure think he's getting ready to persuade you into talking. You know Jerome you really could've saved yourself from having to be put through this by just answering my questions, so now your only recourse is to talk if I was you."

"All right Jerome where would you like it the head or the mouth?" Replied B.J.

"You're some kind of sick fuck; get that gun away from me I'm a federal agent God Dam it."

"Are you kidding me; you're a piece of shit to me Givens; Now Talk!" With the gun pressed to his temple B.J. Starts counting backwards from five clicking the gun into the first open chamber.

"Get that Fucking gun away from me B.J. It wasn't my idea to plant those drugs in your lockers."

"So, who's was it then come on Jerome spill it my fingers starting to itch." Clicking the gun into the next empty open chamber causes Givens to scream out. "TEX! Jesus B.J. McKenna said that if I didn't do what he said he'd kill me," Sweating with my cousin's gun to his head B.J. Next exclaimed.

"So like a dumb fuck you bought into his treat huh, that's being a typical wimp I always knew you were?" "Easy Cuz; your enjoying this a little too much."

"Sorry Eddie your right I am; all right Jerome tell us about the sheriff here now. Did you set him up?" "What do you think?"

"What I think Jerome is you best answer the question I just asked you before my finger starts itching again."

"I admit it Yes; Yes, I set up the sheriff all right now get that gun away from my head!" As much as we wanted to believe him B.J. And I still wasn't convinced so after another empty chamber clicks from his gun.

"Jesus Eddie stop him huh I told you the truth."

"I could Jerome, but I don't know my cousin still needs more convincing I guess, so why don't you tell us everything you know like who master minded this escape of Escabar anyway was it him?" Fearful for his existence we observed Givens shaken his head.

"Tex told me his daughter was being ear marked back then to die in a car explosion if he didn't help Escabar escape Bellevue Hospital."

"So Tex had to get the ball rolling huh?"

"Yes, during a tour he switched Escabar's medical records with another patient who died recently, and he blackmailed one of the staff to put that body in Escabar's bed, and lit it on fire on the bed springs causing a diversion to happen."

"Keep going; What happened next?" I asked while B.J. could be seen pulling the gun slightly away from Jerome's head.

"McKenna next had a laundry truck waiting for Escabar's escape and in the confusion Max vanished from there," Nodding his head B.J. put away his revolver.

"That pretty much confirms what we know already Jerome, so go on continue tell us what happened to Escabar after he escaped?"

Before continuing however Givens got up to lock the office door before seating himself again this time in front of the desk.

"Excuse me I just didn't want somebody walking in on us; Tex did mention what happened after Escabar escaped but you guys won't believe it?"

"Try us Jerome come on."

"All right McKenna said to me Escabar just went underground until the heat died down." "Or the authorities closed the case figuring their investigation went cold isn't that right?" "Yes, that's right"

"All right then what happened?"

"Well according to Tex; Escabar resurfaced back in the summer of 1987 when he started abducted his first victims out in California slowly at first, so not to get rediscovered again, but when he found a system where he wasn't; then he escalated his abductions to other states across the country."

"Some System; a weird one lined message with glued on letters only saying One more added to the fold; along with a head to toe nude photograph in an oversized manila envelope of each of the victims that's some system?"

"Sure is; it still confuses authorities without any evidence of the crime having been committed," "Until now; So where is his hideout located?"

"Honestly I don't know?" Up until now everything he had said pretty much confirmed what we already knew about Escabar, now my only question was why he was lying.

"Come on Jerome; you expect us to believe you don't know; then why were you relocated here from Boston then?"

"B.J. you should know more than anybody we get assigned to some weird places I don't know maybe Tex just wanted me up here to replace the sheriff and be someone who wouldn't go poking around asking questions you tell me?"

"Hold it B.J. I can see this happening, because I know Kenny pretty well and if anything, he is thorough, so that might explain Given reassignment here."

Without Jerome knowing Escabar's hideout I figured we had gotten as much information out of him, so after listening to B.J. reading him his Marinade rights.

He then took from Given's his badge and gun then locked him in a cell.

"All right we got this cock roach now what?"

B.J. replied over to me as I sat down in front of the desk.

"Well, you're going to stay here; while I go pick Kenny up; bring him back here then obviously I'll pick you up. But do me a favor while I'm gone?"

"Sure what?" .... "Play nice."

With that having been said we smiled toward each other, as I next could be seen leaving the sheriff's office. The time now as I could be seen leaving was just after nine o' clock in the morning.

I had to admit however even though we had Jake in protective custody my gut still told me that Jerome wasn't going to be a problem anymore having turned him like we had.

Loyalty was one thing but agreeing to help someone commit felony after felony just because he threatens your life is; being the dumbest of dumb fucks excuse my French.

Seeing Elvis behind the bar; as I walked back in we then nodded toward each other.

"Hey Eddie; Welcome back."

"Thanks Elvis; So, How's Jake doing?"

"Jake's doing great; Snake's babysitting him downstairs along with Kenny, so tell me what happened with your encounter with Givens?" Naturally it wouldn't be until pouring me a cup of coffee then presenting it to me did I begin to enlighten my kid brother on our progress.

"Slow at first; as I entered the office he was doing paperwork if you can believe that still trying his best to play the roll and not doing a very good job of it."

"I'll bet; so, what happened next?"

"Oh, I pulled out the recorder and played him the tape of his conversation with Tex admitting to not only setting up Kenny but B.J. As well."

"Did he say anything smug after hearing that?"

"Nope; for the first time, he didn't have anything to say; but then his jaw literally dropped when B.J. Waltzed in through the back door."

"Oh Boy; I bet that encounter went over like fireworks on the fourth of July huh?"

"Actually, your cousin played it extremely cool; that's of course until I told him that Givens didn't have anything to say to me."

"Then what happened?"

"You're not going to believe me, but after hearing that he empties his gun and only puts back into it one bullet after which he spun the chamber."

"Oh no he didn't do what I'm thinking he did?"

"Yep he sure did holding it up to his temple threatening to shoot him in a Russian roulette situation." I next finished explaining to him everything that Given had said to us concerning not only Escabar, but McKenna also.

"So McKenna's daughter was being ear marked to die if he didn't help Escabar huh?"

"Looks that way little brother."

"To bad Tex is in it good now with aiding and abiding a known fugitive, kidnapping and false imprisonment."

"That's right Elvis exactly but don't forget the obstruction of justice charges there certainly looking at some serious time."

"Hell Yeah; Well now what?" Stopping to contemplate our next move with no real direction in site of locating Escabar. I immediately decided to re-group everyone back at the sheriff's office.

It didn't take Elvis long in finding someone to take over the duties of watching Jake for us, but as we were in the process of leaving with Snake and Kenny.

B.J. was on the telephone back at the sheriff's office bringing his Dad up to date on our investigation. "So dad that's pretty much where we are now."

"Well that's certainly good news son; just too bad Givens couldn't have given you any lead into Escabar's location."

"Yeah well, I'm sure we will be finding him any day now; oh, by the way while I still have you take this down."

"O.K. Son shoot."

"Boston Harbor; Dock 38; Pier 44 a ship left last night around midnight with three metal storage containers on board, I was wondering if you could have your friends at the coast guard and the C.I.A. check it out for us."

"Sure thing; Why do you have a hunch or something?"

"Yeah dad a big one we believe it's shipping three hundred slaves to Singapore. Just thought maybe your friends could intercept it and give it a going over."

"All right got It; I'll be in touch with you once I hear back from them." With that having been relayed they hung up with each other, as B.J. now places his feet up on the corner of Kenny's desk.

Smiling to himself as he continued sitting there my cousin took himself on a sentimental flashback. Where he saw himself back on the football field with his team mates in the fourth quarter of a

pivotal game with 20 seconds left to play.

Defending their goal against their opponent on the Bellingham ten-yard line it was 3rd down and goal.

The ball snaps quickly to the Quarterbacks hands and B.J. hits the center head on spinning to his left he Runs full speed past him sacking the Q.B. Knocking him back ten more yards.

The time was now 10:30a.m. Before we arrived back at Kenny's office.

Smiling as we walked in seeing B.J. Pouring himself a coffee we all patted him on the shoulder, as Elvis and I could be seen passing him to look in on the prisoner.

"Hope you're getting used to your new surroundings special agent Givens?"

"All right Elvis come on; let's leave him alone; come on this isn't getting us nowhere," "Your right; I'm sorry it's just."

"I know little brother; come on." As I lead him away from the holding cell I felt a firmness in my brother's arm.

"Wait; stop here?" Looking at me perplexed now Elvis stares watching me.

"All right; Close your eyes; bend your knees and roll your shoulders ten times forward then backwards for another ten times come on." Hesitating at first, I finally watched him as he begins doing it.

"That a boy Elvis that's right; let that stress roll of you; good can you feel it?

"Yes, I can this is great."

"That's all it takes; it's what I do when it comes to reliving stress." Patting him on the shoulder we turn back to the others.

"Say Eddie; before I forget called my dad to bring him up to date on the case so I hope you don't mind?" "Really well thanks Beatle I appreciate it."

"Your Welcome Cuz; I also mentioned to him about that suspected ship that departed Boston Harbor late last night."

"Yeah?"

"Yeah, and he said to me that he'd have some friends of his check it out for us."

"O.K. Well, at least we got that covered." Sitting down now with a cup of coffee myself; we all waited word from Uncle Jesse on just what his friends discovered.

Meanwhile Escabar was just receiving the horrible news himself by his number one Alexander.

"I Simply cannot believe the incompetence of Jake crashing his rig and dying or for that matter Givens getting himself arrested."

"Well Master then you're really not going to like this piece of news I have for you either.". "Alexander please there's more?"

"Yes Master; I'm sorry to say this but your latest shipment was ah seized by the coast guard out in international waters."

"Idiots; The whole crew are a bunch of idiots in my opinion."

"Yes; Yes Master; they sure are; ah what would you advise me about this situation?"

Annoyed beyond words Escabar turns his back to Alexander momentarily not in disgust of him; so much, but of all the bad news he had reported to him.

But as Escabar was trying to think of some advice to give his young number one. We were however back in the sheriff's office getting the good news ourselves straight from Uncle Jesse himself.

"All right dad; I got you on speaker phone go ahead and repeat what you just said to me please." Clearing his voice Uncle Jesse next could be heard exclaiming to us.

"At approximately 11:20a.m. This morning two coast guard helicopters spotted the suspected vessel traveling west in the South China sea toward the southernmost tip of Singapore. Then at approximately 12:30p.m. Two more Coast Guard ships caught up to them to immediately seize and then board that vessel without incident."

"That sure is weird?"

"Weird Eddie How so?"

"Well with that kind of a cargo on board you'd think the crew would've put up more of a fight to prevent them from being over taken." Without anyone else saying to much about the previous statement it only meant that indeed I was right in my previous assessment.

"Who really knows why they didn't resist possibly they were under orders not to but you mustn't forget about this sick sadistic monster you're dealing with here he could've planned this whole set up to piss off this so-called Mistress Katrina."

"Yes, he could've but why?"

"Who really knows Eddie maybe this individual just wanted to get his rocks off."

"Right B.J. absolutely that sounds about right knowing Maxi like I do." Exclaimed Uncle Jesse.

Then within the silence of the office came the sound of a strange beep.

"What's that beeping?" I asked turning toward the others.

"It's not me?" Answered B.J. Back to us. "Dam, it's me guy's; it's one of my patrols checking in with me." Replied my brother embarrassed at first.

Watching him we next see him answering it.

"This is Elvis; Go ahead."

"Elvis; This is Reggie were out here in the south east portion of the woods oh about 12 miles away from Sable Mountain when my patrol came upon a dead body out here."

"A dead body?"

"Yep; he's dressed in black leather shorts. Boots, and he has criss crossed chains up his chest up and going down his back with two small caliber bullet shots behind his head."

"Sounds like one of the guy's we had that run in before huh Snake?" Nodding his head back to me we next listen as Elvis replies back to Reggie.

"Set up your camp there, and will be in route shortly Elvis out." With that having been said Elvis disconnected with his man now turning to an area map with in the office.

"All right Reggie said he was in the south east portion of the woods 12 miles away from Sable Mountain so here is Sable Mountain that would put Reggie's patrol here." Reconfirming it amongst ourselves Kenny next replies back.

"That's about the same area I lost that truck I was chasing two weeks ago." Turning our heads back to him I next could be heard exclaiming. "Really; how did you lose it?"

"That's the strange thing Eddie it just disappeared while I was right behind it oh about I'd say thirty feet away from it." We then told Kenny of Snake's truck earlier that disappeared in the same way.

"And you were in this vicinity huh?"

"Ah huh; right where your brother's patrol is now exactly." Double checking where he was also pointing to on the map the circumstances. Between where my brother's patrol was, and where Kenny lost his suspected truck was too much coincidental.

The time was now a little bit after 1:30p.m. When Snake, Elvis, and I could be seen rendezvousing with Reggie.

"Eddie think you're you know what will be working by the time we get there?" "Hope so Snake; It sure would give us a better direction to point us into if it did?"

"Huh? Excuse me for being the younger brother here; but just what are you guy's talking about exactly?"

Lost in the cryptic conversation between us Elvis looked toward us completely perplexed, as to what we were discussing.

Naturally it wouldn't be until gently laughing amongst ourselves that I next enlightened my brother of my on again; off again gift I was so blessed with having.

"Awesome; so, you mean you can just touch somebody or anything and see things that's cool big brother?"

"Sometimes Elvis yes, I can, but promise me now that you know I'm holding you to keeping this secret you cannot tell a living soul without my permission is that clear?" Nodding his head, he silently swore to keep my secret to himself.

CHAPTER NINE

T he time now was just going on 2:30p.m. Before we spotted Reggie standing up just ahead of us.

We brought everything we could think of; not really knowing just what to expect.

But like Uncle Jesse always used to tell me better to have it with you than to regret not having it at all.

"Hi Elvis, it's over here come on?' Exclaimed Reggie guiding us over to the body.

"Dose this look like one of the guy's You confronted before?" Asked Elvis watching Snake and I nodding our heads in agreement that it was one of the men.

"Ah huh; He is one of them all right." It wouldn't be until after carefully explaining to Reggie that we now needed some privacy that he appeared to understand and then left us there.

"All right Elvis here goes." After taken three deep breaths I next placed my hands upon the individual's chest then began to see the images there playing themselves out before me.

The first image showed a black van entering a mountain; next it showed from there that very same vehicle descending in what looked like an elevator.

After which the scene switched showing a storage room of some type with various boxes stacked on top of each other.

The fourth image showed partially to fully nude women being lead around by other men dressed like this one.

The last and final image now showed out of sequence; that this before mentioned mountain was that one we were presently 12 miles away from.

Completely exhausted now it took me again several minutes before I could tell Snake and Elvis what I had indeed seen in my visions.

"Well I know a little more to what's going on now thanks to this guy here." "Don't hold us in suspense big brother: Come on big brother tell us?"

"All right Elvis; First thing I saw was a black van entering a mountain; Then I saw this vehicle descending in an elevator somehow; After that I saw a warehouse; Then I saw boxes stacked on top of each other. I then witnessed partially to full nude women being led around by guy's like this one here; oh, and the good news it's that mountain there," Snake and Elvis turned in the direction of Sable Mountain.

"You mean Brenda and Lori-Ann is in there! Asked Elvis shaking with anticipation of reuniting with his abducted love as was I.

"Correction Elvis they are not in there to be exact; they are beneath it somewhere; now all we have to do is figure out a way to get inside." I knew that though charging in would've been my brother's first option.

It certainly wasn't mine give the fact that the women would've been killed if we went in halfcocked. No, my plan now believe it or not was to regroup first and develop a workable plan of action. But as we were gathering the others to head back into town; Uncle Jesse however was back in Boston having a very enlightened conversation with Tex McKenna.

"This is an outrage Jesse; How dare you arrest me for what?"

"You honestly asking me that huh? Excuse me but would you kindly listen to this please?" Placing the cassette recorder down in front of him Uncle Jesse pushes the play button.

"Have you had a chance to count the money I gave you earlier?" "I'm counting it now as a matter of fact." "Good I'm glad hope it's all there?"

"Yeah me too; but to tell you the truth I do owe you an apology for what I said to you earlier."

"Forget it Tex; I mean if someone just given me fifty thousand dollars for my two nieces and then proceeded to show me what I showed you earlier trust me I would've called that guy a sick pervert too." Popping that tape out Uncle Jesse replaces it with a second one after which he then pushes play once again.

"Sheriff's office; can I help you?"

"This is Tex McKenna get me Agent Givens please."

"Good morning boss thought you'd call me sooner or later; What's up?"

"Just got back from a meeting; thought I'd check in on your situation where your located care to give me a report yet?"

"Well I'm happy to report the sheriff has been dealt with,"

"That's great news; whew; now we all can breathe a sigh of relief thank you Jerome." "You're welcome boss; so, tell me how did your meeting go?"

"It went as well as expected our benefactor got his list, and I got myself paid as usual for it with incentives."

"Gotta love them huh; so, do you suspect he'll be contacting you?"

"Can't say for sure maybe; yes." Once more Uncle Jesse's finger shuts off the small cassette player. "If you think these are the only tapes I have here think again." Carefully he pulls out a second tape and puts it with the first.

"Jesse; I don't know what to say?"

"Try telling me the truth Tex if you can manage it; because weather you know it or not you're in some serious trouble." With a court appointed typographer brought in next she takes her place awaiting to take down McKenna's statement.

But while Uncle Jesse was busy working on the F.B.I. director's confession the time was 2:50p.m.

As Snake, Elvis, and I found ourselves back at the sheriff's office.

"So how did the identification of that guy go?" Asked B.J. standing up as we walked in.

"Great; the identification proved he was one of the guys we confronted yesterday." Slightly suspicious about my lack of details in not being able to supply any more information. I next found myself ushering B.J. out of the office to finish explaining.

"Listen I also had another vision showing me that Escabar was deep below Sable Mountain with his crew and a lot of ladies as his prisoners."

"I knew there was more you weren't telling me."

"Yeah well now that you know; could you somehow get a hold of your dad and tell him about this; so, he can somehow give Kenny a call and run interference on this so I?"

"Hold it; So, you won't have to come out and confess to your buddy about your special gift." "Yeah something like that."

"No problem cuz consider it done." Watching B.J. Walking away I breathed a sigh of relief. Sure, Kenny was my friend and I knew yes, he may of understood if I were to mention it to him; but also, I shouldn't have been so fearful of just what he might of thought about me if he did know. It took some time but roughly around 4:00PM Uncle Jesse did manage to phone Kenny

"Commissioner James; it's an honor hearing from you Sir; ah yes could you hold a minute sir?" It wouldn't be until putting him on speaker that we all could hear him say.

"Hello? Can you hear me now?"

"Loud and clear Uncle Jesse go ahead."

"Well first of all I think I need to inform you boy's that around 2:45p.m. Today I arrested Tex McKenna and had him brought in for questioning; and through the course of the interview he after a while did confirm that he not only aided Maxwell Escabar, but through being blackmailed by him assisted in supplying him with various lists of women and young ladies."

"Awesome dad did he say anything else?"

"Yes, as a matter of fact he confessed to setting you up with those small plastic baggies of cocaine along with Agent Givens; So, you're off the hook son."

"He next confessed to me about this meeting he had with Escabar where he witnessed Lori-Ann getting bound, blindfolded, and then getting if you can believe this tickle tortured. Sorry those are his words there before him beneath of all places Sable Mountain; Kenny isn't that near you somewhere up there?"

'Yes, it is commissioner James, it's very close by to us."

"Well that's what Tex confessed to me in a sworn statement he made a little while ago; that's where Escabar is with his men and thousands of those missing victims; so, my next question to you gentlemen is just what are you going to do about it?" Seen smiling to myself after hearing that odd question posed I then exclaimed back.

"Everything and anything in our power Uncle Jesse to see that justice is served in true James Boy fashion."

"That a boy Eddie well said. Tell me though how many do you have up there that will be helping you; the four of you right?"

"Yes Uncle Jesse that's right."

"Well give me your fax number because I have a surprise to send you boy's."

Suspicious as to just what this surprise could be I gave him the fax number after which we next see signed documents coming out over the fax machine.

"Hope these will help you their compliments of his honor the Mayor had lunch today with him." Smiling amongst ourselves his honor had indeed drafted up four special documents granting each of us cart blanch to bring in this maniac in no matter what the cost.

"Thank you, Uncle Jesse, and please if you speak to his honor again could you thank him for us also tell him we really appreciate this."

"Sure, I'll tell him that; but remember Eddie when you do happen to bring Escabar in; it certainly won't be you appreciating what the Mayor has done; as much as this country will for what you're about to do remember that all of you and good hunting." And with that having been said we hung up our respected phones.

"So now what big brother?"

"Now we go back to where that body was found and come up with a way of getting into that mountain." Snake and I stayed with Kenny; While Elvis and B.J. went to round up a few more guys to bring with us.

The time now was 5:45p.m. Before our selected teams could be re-assembled up where Reggie had found that body before.

B.J. took his team and set up their camp to the east, Snake likewise took his team and set up his camp in the west, While I stayed at the base camp to the north of the mountain; Elvis took his to the south to set up their base.

"Command to all leader's report?"

"Team 1 Set up ready to rock."

"Team 2 set up ready to rock"

"Team 3 Locked Loaded and ready to roll."

"Command to team 3; Leave it to you little brother to just be a tad different, all right team leaders let's hunt then down. Keep your eyes and ears open and report anything unusual during your patrols command out." As I placed the radio down my adrenaline started pumping faster as the sounds of the night took center stage.

The first several hours kept producing nothing in the way of intelligence from any of the teams, but just when we had given up any possibility of packing it up, and in for the night. Elvis came through first the time was 8:00p.m.

"Team three to command; Team three to command; We spotted three tractor trailer trucks just passing us on the south side heading to the mountain over."

"Fantastic job Elvis; you hear him boy's let's roll south side command out."

Taken several minutes before we actually arrived there Elvis in true James boy fashion held his point. "Awesome job little brother I'm proud of you."

"Thanks Eddie; they went over there stopped pulled down one of those tree branches and then drove into the mountain there."

"Must be a secret mechanism of some kind that activate the mountains opening?" B.J. exclaimed back to the rest of us.

"Sounds like it beetles for sure; Say Snake would you care to take a couple of my brother's ninja's and do a little recon for me?" Watching him pulling down his mask Snake next could be seen silently pointing to three of my brother's ninjas to follow him as he leads the way straight into the darkness.

"Team two to command; team two to command; The coast is clear; I repeat the coast is clear; they had three sentries here; but we swiftly neutralized them."

"Good work Snake; hold your position were coming in; command out." Quietly the rest of us could be seen moving up.

"Now comes the fun part; Snake I'd like you and B.J. to go ahead of us with your teams and find as many victims as you can and get them out."

"Excuse me for asking this cuz; but does that mean that Elvis and you will be in there also locating Brenda and Lori-Ann."

"It doses why?"

"Oh no reason it's just; be careful huh from what my dad said to us before this guy's dangerous." "Thanks, beatle for your concern Elvis and I appreciate it but I really have to correct you on something;

When your dad said Maxi was dangerous he might have left out one thing from that statement." "Huh? What's that?"

"Your dad left your cousin and I out of that equation." With that having been said B.J. for the first time watched his cousin and I displaying a collective James Boy stare. And God help that someone who thought they'd deny either of us this time what was rightfully ours.

My brother and I continued waiting patiently as they took the elevator down first with their men. "Wow; my stomach feels queasy." Having had that feeling in my own life once or twice before I smiled to myself as I next replied back.

"I had that feeling before myself in the past."

"Really? Well what is it; because it sure feels weird to me?"

"It's something I call butterflies used to get them before all of my matches." "So, dose it goes away?"

"Absolutely little brother as fast as it came upon you it will subside." "Whew; that's good to know thanks big brother." "You're welcome Elvis anytime,"

"Team three to command; team three to command; Elevators coming up for you see you inside team three out." Disconnecting from Snake next I picked out two ninjas to remain here at the entrance while the rest of us went into the belly of the beast.

"All right little brother it's officially ShowTime hope you brought your rock n' roll shoes?" Watching him nodding his head smiling over to me we let the other men enter first before getting into the elevator last.

"All right men your job will be to assist the other teams in extracting as many victims as possible; watch your backs; kick ass only when necessary; but pay attention to this please if you see Escabar do not engage him simply watch and report his where about; he's ours to deal with." Together my brother and I smiled to one another as we allowed the others to exit the elevator first.

Like in my vision before Elvis and I found ourselves walking cautiously down the lengthy hallway of all places what looked like that warehouse in my vision.

"This must seem like de'ja'vu for you huh big brother?"

"Just keep your eyes open Elvis, but to answer your question; yes, it sure dose." Several minutes pass after leaving that warehouse before we encounter three of Escabar's men.

Side stepping the first man coming out of the room to his left; Elvis watched as I clothes lined the bastard's ass, before the second man came out.

With fists flying Elvis could be seen ducking and dodging his attacker's hands with his speed. Then once an opening had presented itself to Elvis; he let his attacker feel the stings of his two spin kicks knocking that one completely out.

The third man and I however were engaging one another in a battle to see who'd win. Too bad as I broke his arm catching it over my shoulder. And then hitting him with a stiff gut shot that my man feel backwards after kicking him in the face as he went down.

Giving each other a high five we continued our search for Maxi. Passing various rooms with unconscious men inside tied and gaged left there only meant that my brother's men were doing their jobs quite well.

Escabar's secret world here was truly perverse if his victims weren't being tickle tortured in his numerous sadistic restraints. His victims were used in other rooms for his pornographic films completely unaware of their involvement.

"Talk about a sick mother; huh big brother?"

"Ah huh you can say that; he sure is." Carefully as we walked about one of his observation rooms with a full view of the completely different apparatuses that his men used in the ajasoned room.

"Eddie come here a second check this out?" Walking over I see Elvis holding up a manifest with the three hundred names of the victims that already had been rescued earlier in the South China sea.

"Excellent work Elvis, this looks like a detailed list of the names of the three hundred women." Still looking at the document I was holding Elvis however could be seen picking up something else up of the floor.

"Hey Eddie check this one out it looks like a contract between this Singaporean Mistress and Escabar for wholly molly fifty thousand dollars for three hundred slaves." Together we looked at one another each thinking to ourselves the same thing.

"Talk about an investment paying off dividends."

"You said it; Where did you find this exactly?"

"Over there beside that folder on the floor." Leaning down to pick it up; it flopped open to reveal the photographs of those various women on the list I still had in my hand.

"Jackpot."

"Nothing like a little more evidence to cinch the hook in Maxi's mouth a little deeper." Without anything else to uncover my brother and I left heading back into the corridor.

"Team two to command; Team two to command mission accomplished; the men my team confronted have been dealt with and their victims have been extracted from beneath the mountain over."

"Command to team two great work cuz; tell your team awesome job well done. Have you heard from Snake yet?"

"No not yet; hey do you think I should call in the cavalry yet?"

"That's a rodger beatle; go for it; command out." Not really worrying about Snake checking in with any of us yet Elvis and I continued searching for Escabar.

The time now was just going on 9:00p.m. Before we spotted Snake and his men leading out the last of the victims.

Turning over the file we still had over to him I instructed him to give It to my Uncle if he was there.

Not thinking he wouldn't be I had faith he would upon Escabar's capture.

"Well now that we turned the evidence over to Snake now what?"

"Let's go this way." Turning to a corridor just to our right we proceeded straight ahead.

"You know something this reuniting like this to rescue our ladies is great and all, but it got me to thinking?"

"About what?"

"About the fact that I haven't asked anyone to be my best man yet at my wedding; So how about it big brother; after we nail this psycho and rescue the women would you do me the honor?"

Stopping momentarily, we next could be seen hugging each other in another tender James boy moment, "I'd be honored thank you for asking me Elvis; but listen you got to do me a favor though?"

"Which is?

"When we do confront Maxi, you won't kill him like you originally planned, remember our first breakfast together?"

"Yes of course I remember that, all right you got a deal; I won't kill him." As we continued walking we passed other rooms until we came to another large wooden door.

"Great now what big brother? should we knock." Assessing the situation momentarily, I came to the conclusion that indeed this was the last unchecked room.

"Well given the fact it hasn't been checked what the heck why not?" Together Elvis and I did it right in true James Boy fashion with a thunderous side kick that knocked the door down completely off its hinges.

"KNOCK; KNOCK." Ordinarily a normal side kick put to a large wooden door would've broken both our legs in our first attempt like this, but taken into consideration that my brother and I were extremely pissed together with our adrenaline being pumped to the max—(No pun intended) we each breathed a sigh of relief it actually worked the first time.

"Holly shit we actually did it."

"Yeah we did it; be cool now." I replied back to him as we continued standing there just watching Maxi atop of his throne. Positioned to either side of him were Brenda and Lori-Ann.

"Gentlemen; come in we've been expecting you." Smiling his smuggest smile he appeared like most maniacs did in the movies thinking he had the upper hand, but he certainly didn't figure that I had an equalizer. "Listen to this; Snake, the boys activated their trackers along with their walkie talkies, its Escabar." Carefully watching the receiver, he held in his hand Snake see's out exact position blinking.

"There a hundred yards in; come on B.J.; You three ninja's come with us to,"

Snake exclaimed leading them back into the mountain. But as they were making their way back in; Elvis and I continued holding our stances.

"Listen up Maxi; were not here on some damn social visit; so, you can cut the Bullshit your slinging; just give up; because your though. Oh, and those ladies up there with you their coming with us," Nodding his head back in confirmation was Elvis looking back at me completely impressed with my speech.

But before Maxi could come back with a rhetorical response of his own there out of the corner came two small smoke pellets thrown at both Brenda and Lori-Ann.

Blinded to what was happening he never saw my brother's ninja's coming into whisk both girls off to safety.

Only after the smoke had cleared itself did Escabar realize what had just occurred.

"You may have your ladies back now; but if you think I'm going to be taking in, or back to Bellevue you're in for a much bigger disappointment gentlemen?"

Exactly like the girls had done before Escabar to threw down a smoke pellet making his escape under its veil.

"Gee that was theatrical to say the least."

"Sure was; Listen go back check on the girls; and tell Snake and B.J. what happened; I'm going after Escabar."

"Oh no not without me you're not; we started this thing together and if you're going after him I'm backing you up big brother let's go." Smiling over to him it certainly became pretty obvious; he was right.

After giving that room a thorough once over in search for clues to where he could've disappeared my brother and I next thought to ourselves a little James Boy interrogation 101 was called for. Walking briskly we aggressively entered another room to find one of Escabar's henchmen still tied and gagged.

"Get him up; we haven't got much time." Watching Elvis picking up that man together we placed him hard into a chair before moving his gag under his chin.

"What's your name?" A normal interrogation certainly wouldn't have either of us smacking this guy hard up the back of his head like we were, but like I mentioned before this was James Boy interrogation.

"Alex, Alexander," The man replied.

"All right Alexander, my brother and I as you see are not patient, so were going to ask you a question about your boss".

"If you tell us the truth we just might allow you to live; but if you fuck with us we'll let's just hope for your sake you're not stupid enough to even consider that option." Smiling over toward me; Elvis began asking him first.

"Did your boss ever discuss his escape plan with you!" Carefully we watched him trying his best to stall us; but after a couple of well-timed whacks upside of his head my brother and I got him back talking.

"Jesus Christ, enough with the hitting, huh! I'm thinking, I remember him telling me about a secret airstrip just over the Canadian border." Looking back to each other my brother and I certainly thought the same thing next.

"Shit if he makes that strip?"

"Yeah, I know he could go anywhere his heart desires at that point." "You got that right."

"All right Alex; say My brother and I do believe you; and you are telling us the truth; what kind of vehicle did he use to escape in?" Watching him closing his eyes at least this time he was quicker in answering back. "All right I'll tell you not that you two hot shots are going to be able to stop him now!" Looking at him my brother first grabbed him with a very nasty neck pinch we watched him wincing in pain, as I leant down to answer.

"Alex remember what I said to you about fucking with us before, well if you'd rather have my brother continue with that painful procedure he has you in keep stalling us, but if you'd rather this pain stop then I'd seriously suggest you tell us about this vehicle Escabar's getting away in." Still wincing as he was Elvis and I watched him next agreeing to talk.

"Jesus, fuck! that pressure point thing of your brothers hurts like a son-of-a-bitch"

"Glad you like it; but now like my brother suggested talk or I'll put you back into it longer?" Still watching him trying to get the blood flowing again he next said to us.

"No that's quite all right Mr. James I kind of like the feel of being able to move my neck again. The vehicle my master escaped in is called a Tumbler."

"I've heard of those there small like an A.T.V. They were used in the war to carry cables across re veins and bridges, right?"

"Yes, Mr., James that's correct." Sensing he was indeed telling us the truth we could be seen leaving him still tied up.

"A tumbler huh; I saw something about them being indestructible is that right Eddie?"

"Practically, afraid so; but that's not to say it can't be stopped." Seen coming out of the mountain now; as I predicted before there was Uncle Jesse standing next to Kenny.

CHAPTER TEN

Meanwhile back at the staging area Lori-Ann was just coming out of Escabar's hypnotic control.

"What the? Hi; Hi Snake; Where's Eddie?" She said looking at him.

Listening she hears Snake explaining my plan to stop Escabar; naturally leaving out the most horrific part from it.

After giving the others news about Escabar's escape I next could be heard briefly explaining my plan to stop him. Which by the looks upon the faces of those around me could indeed be felt.

"Let me see if I get this straight your telling me your going up in my helicopter flying over this tumbler contraption to jump out and hopefully grab on to this thing; then place a quarter stick of C-4 to its inner wheel hub while this thing is still in motion?"

"That's the extended version of the plan yeah Uncle Jesse." Knowing me like he did as we continued walking toward the chopper he knew by my expression that there was really no stopping me. Popping his head out from the passenger's seat was Elvis already buckled into the seat.

"Hi Eddie; I'd like you to meet our pilot here Chet; Chet this is my big brother Eddie." Giving Elvis a serious look he continued smiling, as Chet and I shook hands upon meeting one another.

"Chet's my best pilot Eddie been flying birds since Nam He'll take good care of you both. Chet; Eddie's calling the shots here listen to him and bring them both back alive huh?" Nodding his head with a thumb up we listen as he says back to Uncle Jesse.

"Not to worry Commissioner I'll take good care of your boy's here; All right boys hold on." Feeling the chopper lifting off the ground I tried my best not to show I was scared to death.

"Consider yourself lucky Little brother you being strapped into your seat the way you are." "Huh; why's that?"

"Because if you weren't I'd kick your ass for being here that's why; What are you thinking about coming with me for?"

"Consider it moral support; besides I figured you'd need an extra hand to help you with that harness; and no disrespect to Chet here being the pilot and all.

Having to fly this bird; but I just couldn't see him helping you out and having to do that also." Even though I may not have wanted my brother here I certainly couldn't have argued the fact he was right about needing help with the harness and the c-4. So, after kneeling back away from him I next could be seen behind Chet to start meditating.

The whirling sounds of the props spinning couldn't be heard as I saw myself sitting there. Visualizing the jump most of the time placed me in a mental zone as I saw myself landing on it. From there I saw myself pushing the start timer that was already pre-set for 3:00 minutes to the C4 bar. After which I saw myself firmly attaching it next to the right inner wheel hub seconds before being lifted off of it by Chet. It may have been one thing to be scared like I was; but it was another just to let this maniac get away with what he's done. But as I continued replaying those events in my mind my eyes only sure of what I needed to do popped themselves back open once more completely re-focused on my pending task at hand. Showing absolutely no outward fear my brother assisted me with getting the harness on. Once I felt its snugness. I next then pre-set the c-4's timer for its required three minutes before then being seen getting out on the ledge of the chopper; as the wind gusted passed me my facial expression was one of complete seriousness as the choppers light spotted Escabar's tumbler. 100ft directly in front of us.

"Eddie the boarders estimated to be 100miles away, so we just might get a second chance at this lunatic before he crosses the Canadian border."

"Understood little brother I know what you're saying; but I'm not going to miss this first attempt to nail this; Chet how close is he now?

"75 feet away and coming up quick; get ready when I say go jump." The Tumbler began swiftly coming up to us before Chet screamed "Go Go"

Letting go of the chopper I felt my feet next leaving the safety of the chopper's railing until I saw myself landing hard catching its right edge of the still moving machine.

"He just caught the rear of it but he made it Chet he's on it!" It might not have been how I visualized landing But at least I was on it. Seeing it's inner wheel hub in front of me. I next hit the start mechanism activating its timer after which I finally attached the quarter stick of C4 explosive as planned above the inner wheel hub.

Just seconds before grabbing the harness cable; as I saw myself letting go of the tumblers right edge simply watching it as it continued on its way.

Listening to hear the explosion it the distance as we continued inwrought.

Having flipped itself over miles up from where we were the choppers search light spotted it just up ahead. As we made our way up to it fast. After releasing the cable, I saw myself dropping down safely 5ft off the ground.

Whoever designed this thing knew big time what they were doing aside from a couple of dings this thing looked indestructible however still seeing our prisoner in there trapped caused me to smile as Chet and Elvis could be seen running up to join me.

"Holly Shit Eddie that was some jump you made; wow I'm glad I was around to see it." He exclaimed as he threw his arms around me.

"Thanks Elvis I appreciate the compliment; but little brother I'm happy to report to you that's about the only time I'll be attempting anything like that in the near future." And with that having been said we next could be seen waiting for Chet to join us.

"Sorry about the delay in getting out here with you Eddie; just had to call the Calvary with our exact location they'll be here within ten minutes." Smiling toward each other at least that was good to hear.

It took us several minutes before the three of us could be seen pulling out from beneath that tumbler of his; the 6'4" frame of Maxwell Escabar which as we were in the process of doing he then let out the most hellish scream.

"Son-of-a-fucking-bitch can't you do gooders pull anyone out of something without trying to kill them!" Smiling back toward each other Elvis next says.

"Believe me Escabar if that were the case you certainly wouldn't be breathing so if I were you I'd shut the fuck up before something dose happen."

Seen walking away at the same time; Elvis just glares down disgusted at our prisoner for the anguish he caused

"Wow Maxi that's some little brother I have there huh; telling you off like that but you know something if I were you I'd be listening right about now to him unless of course you'd rather him come back here to personally shut you up,"

Nodding his head back over to me I nodded mine back as well to him.

"We'd certainly hate to be the bearers of bad news; but you know your boys McKenna and his little fart special agent Givens are both done, there in custody as we speak behind bars just like you're going to be soon as the authorities cart your sorry ass off."

"Oh and that ship that left Boston harbor late last night was seized earlier today and boarded by the United State Coast Guard in international waters out near the South China Sea. It's crew all were placed under arrest, But the prisoners I'm happy to inform you that they we're carrying were all released and returned to their loved ones."

Suddenly as we continued standing there staring at him we then heard in the distance sounds of two apache helicopters making their approach from the western sky.

"Hear that Max; listen can you hear them; it's the authorities coming to arrest that sick sadistic ass of yours for every crime you and your goons committed".

Not sure why, I took hold of Elvis's arm to gently lead him away from Escabar.

Knowing pretty much his adrenaline had kicked itself in any further he just might have done something actually that we'd both be regretting as those choppers kept approaching us.

"Thanks a lot Eddie for doing that back there; I almost saw myself loosing it."

"I know Elvis that's why I did it; besides Uncle Jesse always said to me that there's a time to hit somebody and a time to let it go; this just happens to be one of those times."

As we both stood there smiling; at each other Elvis's smile could be seen getting wider as he then see's Brenda being helped down off the first chopper.

While I continued standing there just being a witness to each of them reuniting there. I knew it certainly wouldn't be long after that when Lori-Ann and I would see each other next. The medical technicians were the first on the scene followed by B.J. Uncle Jesse, and Snake, as the three of us carefully watched them tending to Escabar.

Listening to hear Escabar in addition to those two broken legs had himself three cracked ribs on top of that certainly wasn't going to cause any of us to shed a tear for him giving the anguish he put us all through. So together we just stood there watching without any facial expression upon any of our faces; as the technicians continued working to secure him to the choppers stretcher; and his eventual flight back to Boston.

Several additional minutes passed shortly after giving Uncle Jesse my account of the events prior to us capturing Escabar did I then view Lori-Ann being helped out of the third chopper that had just landed. Seen dressed in a two-piece bikini together with a single tear flowing down each of our cheeks. We next could be seen briskly walking toward each other. Seconds after jumping into my waiting arms; did the two of us kiss the other with the burning blazes of passion re-lighting themselves back within our hearts once more.

"Thank God your all right; I missed you so much."

"Feelings mutual honey I've missed you too; but never mind me I'm fine; question is being you, are you all right? Did he hurt you?"

"No, not that I can remember; I don't think he did; to tell you the truth baby I can't remember to much about this whole ordeal really."

"Ok honey it's all right I'm just happy your here in my arms so I'm not going to force you if you can't remember; you can't remember." Suddenly within that moment as we kissed each other once more; time froze itself there for us.

Feeling her ankles locked beneath me as well as her sensuous body pressed firmly against me there.

I dared anyone with a crowbar to try and break us apart from this powerful embrace.

Carefully watching after getting herself down off of me I took her hand so together we could be seen reunited walking over to the others.

"Lori-Ann; sweety how are you?" Exclaimed Uncle Jesse standing there next to the others.

"Much better now Uncle Jesse thank you for asking." Smiling together I next watch them hugging each other.

After which I felt Lori-Ann's hand sneaking itself into mine once more as we smiled back at one another. Elvis and I however gave the rest of them all a full run down of the events prior to Maxi's apprehension.

"I knew Snake left something out of his explanation before." Seen next with her head down to the ground I sensed her disappointment in me.

"Listen to me Lori; I apologize for not being the one who told you; but you have to believe me with this maniac escaping I had to think of something fast to stop him before he got away with what he did. You know I love you." Lifting her head slowly our eyes met.

"Guess I can't be mad at you for not telling me; I love you too, but do me a favor?" "Sure absolutely anything name it."

"The next time you think of doing any death defying could you please promise to restrict it to the bedroom where I can see it too?"

"Absolutely; now that's a promise I'll be happy to keep." After which our lips softly met once more sealing the new deal between us.